UP THE SPIRAL STAIRCASE TO THE 4TH DIMENSION

MURIEL GRAVES

Trafford
PUBLISHING™

Books suggested to read
are those by Alice A. Bailey

———————————————

Order this book online at www.trafford.com/07-2620
or email orders@trafford.com

Most Trafford titles are also available at major online book retailers.

Note for Librarians: A cataloguing record for this book is available from Library
and Archives Canada at www.collectionscanada.ca/amicus/index-e.html

Printed in Victoria, BC, Canada.

ISBN: 978-1-4251-5812-5 (sc)
ISBN: 978-1-4251-5813-2 (e)

*Our mission is to efficiently provide the world's finest, most comprehensive
book publishing service, enabling every author to experience success.
To find out how to publish your book, your way, and have it available
worldwide, visit us online at www.trafford.com/10510*

Trafford rev. 8/4/2009

www.trafford.com

North America & international
toll-free: 1 888 232 4444 (USA & Canada)
phone: 250 383 6864 ♦ fax: 250 383 6804

THE GREAT INVOCATION

From the point of light
Within the Mind of God
Let light stream forth into
The minds of men.
Let Light descend on Earth.
From the point of Love
Within the Heart of God
Let love stream forth into
The hearts of men.
May Christ return to Earth.
From the centre where the
Will of God is known
Let purpose guide the little
wills of men -
The purpose which the
Masters know and serve.
From the centre which we
Call the race of men
Let the Plan of Love
And Light work out.
And may it seal the door
Where evil dwells.
Let Light and Love and
Power restore the Plan on earth.

INTRODUCTION

I have been asked, through telepathic communication, to put out a simple philosophy that may help those that are ready to tread the Path. It is a small booklet, but hopefully will give those who are asking the questions Why, Where and When a little illumination.

This booklet has been written through Thought Transference, enabling people to read how The Teachers are able to transmit a further interpretation of the Purpose of Life. Maybe when this is accepted man will ultimately know himself, and also the feeling of inner peace and contentment which is really the Jewel in the Crown

Chapter 1

FINDING MIND

As we journey through this life, how often must we ask 'what is the purpose of it all?' We strive for various achievements, and yet when the time comes to leave we go out with nothing; so surely there must be some reason for the blood, sweat and tears? When suddenly, as we sit quietly and ponder, an answer appears to emerge – Is it a training or learning for some other experience that we have not yet understood? What if this is only the catalyst for a different expression of ourselves? Much like the caterpillar turning into a butterfly, the one does not accept the other, but we know they are the same thing.

Suddenly a new aspect of life begins to creep in and we ask and search for more questions as to what we really are, and why and how this planet exists in the first place. Is each and every one of us playing a part in this great whole (the planet/universe) and we don't really know it? Or do we? Why are we asking these questions? What makes us think? Who am I really? It seems that 'think' is the key word. How does that come about? From the mind? If we open up our head or brain we will not find mind. We cannot touch it or see it but we know it is there. So where is it coming from?

Today we are familiar with computers and so can liken our brain to a computer. But, like the computer, information has to be put into it by us. Hence, mind instructs the brain and this information comes from another dimension altogether – for the sake of identification we will call it the 4th dimension as it is different from the 3rd dimension on which we can see and feel. It is, therefore, a force from outside the body, and it is this force that we gradually recognise and learn to use through meditation and contemplation. It seems, as it enters the brain, that it is pure thought, but it has to be transmitted into the lower mind to become conscious and able to instruct the person on everyday things. We call this intelligence, i.e. how we live in this 3rd dimensional, concrete world and, depending on the quality of that instruction, we are able to use the brain to a greater or lesser degree.

Today we are very interested in intelligence. Tests can be given and an I.Q. can be established. But why are these quotients so different? Could it be dependent upon the ability of the conscious mind to transmit the information to the computer brain? Maybe this is what intelligence really is and why each of us has a different degree of intelligence. Could this also be related to our use of it in a previous life-some people knowing how to use that computer and hence make greater use of it in this life?

Then we ask another question, where has all this information come from in the first place? We have received it from somewhere else. Again we realise in meditation that the source is outside the physical body. We may call it thought, but that idea/information comes from a universal source that we can dip into when we accept/realise that it is there. Thoughts, therefore, are collected (like the antennae of the butterfly) and transformed into the higher self, or sub-conscious, and then the conscious mind. During the journey, unfortunately, they get distorted and we put into operation what we think we have been given. All of us are aware of this; when we know what we really should do we change it and give ourselves a logical explanation as to why we have done this.

Thought is always pure and the higher self, the part of us that is God, in which we live and move and have our being, has a greater chance to hold onto that God-given gift. But it is so delicate, so precious, that it takes the flick of an eyelid and it changes into what we want it to mean, not what the original idea was. Some people do not accept this and think that thought is a logical, 3rd dimensional idea which they have produced; but as we start to ask these questions we have to accept that we are God's children, Gods in the making, and as such will ultimately bring to our conscious mind the true reality of His understanding and realisation.

We occasionally meet people who have an elegance and beauty we cannot explain. They put into practice, not all the time, that form of expression that is direct from the higher self/mind, and seem to know how to direct the thought form in all its purity. Gradually we have to stand back and see ourselves as we really are − self-realisation − finding this out for ourselves, not through psychiatrists or psychologists. In the 21st century the work of Jung will be studied and understood much more; he seemed to relate to this universal pool of the unconscious so much more, and each of us will gradually accept and realise we can drink from it.

On our flight back to the conscious 3rd dimensional world we often lose the instruction and distort the whole idea or purpose of that journey. But as we make the journey more and more it becomes clearer; we know that all we need is there, we are part of IT, we are IT, we can feel the joy of flying about and touching the essence of our Being, understanding eventually where the source of all life really is. To a degree it is like dreaming - we each of us know how often that happens but when we wake it is gone. Sometimes we remember a little bit but eventually, with practice, the whole thing. Then the big question is what does it mean? Here again each of us has to find our own explanation, and even that will unfurl as we make those journeys more often.

A psychologist can only give an explanation in the light of his understanding/evaluation, and seldom can really give you a personal explanation . Each of us is on our own path. We make journeys into this 3rd dimensional world, but like the dream we eventually know how to direct our course, where to find the signposts, read them and follow the instructions, ultimately finding we are back to that universal pool of consciousness called God or Love.

It is all so simple and easy but it takes us so long to get the hang of the thing. Once in this sea of matter we argue and debate and muddle ourselves even more, until one day we seem to hear a voice say 'Be still and silent and you will see/hear God'. Those who have trodden this path many times know this, but even they cannot always believe it.

The 21st Century is the age of the Mind – The Aquarian Age – shown as a man carrying a pitcher. The pitcher is full of the spiritual waters – a dip in the universal sea of existence. It will be that question that the bulk of humanity will be debating, trying to accept the lifeforce and hopefully learning, through meditation, to take our own pitcher, dip it into the sea and carry it back into the existence that we have created at this moment in time. As we journey through the universe/space we collect particles which gradually build us up into a formation of so-called matter. This matter holds a density which evolves into a soul; in order for it to evolve, it needs to find a species to latch onto; sometimes it finds it too difficult and so has to spend longer finding its being, but eventually it gets attracted to a planet. Here we find souls which have the necessary evolution to be caught by a planet – Earth. Just as seeds set in a garden can lie dormant until the rain comes to wake them up and then grow, so the soul lies dormant on the planet until it finds the necessary colour/sound vibration that attracts it to a human. It could be attracted to a plant or animal, but once in that area it will grow and produce the type of Being that is its polarity. So now the soul enters the human and it is, as we call it, born.

Now, according to the evolution of the soul, that will stimulate the computer/brain and so parts of the brain, the speech, sight, feeling, smell, will take on the consciousness of what we call the senses. The more the soul can experience as it goes in and out of that computer/brain, the more it learns to control, and so the Being can use its eyes, hands, ears and mouth, and start to make these senses work to order. All is mechanical at first, but as it gets used to working the Being, then it receives free-will and has to work the brain itself. Many millions of years (so-called) will elapse until the senses become conscious and mind is produced. This changes the mechanical Being into a thought–provoking personality and hence, through the mind, will create a human Being.

The world, as you know it, is on the brink of collapse – not only through Homo sapiens but by the development of the mind elements. Just as man takes his place in the pattern of things, so do the animal, vegetable, and mineral worlds. Hence as the planet Earth moves on its orbit, so too does it move into different vibrations from outer space and these affect the whole dimension and understanding of the creations on this sphere. It is when 'life' becomes difficult that we start to ask ourselves a few deep questions. Answers come from various areas but the key to the whole thing is evolution. If we can stand back and look at ourselves we begin to see a pattern and the tide of evolution starts to give us a little of the picture. Each of the Beings that has established themselves here is governed by this, which in itself can be transformed into sound and colour, for that is what it is truly all about.

We weave our way through colour and create our own rainbow ultimately arriving at the white light – hence the understanding of its true composition. Through meditation, or the silence, we give the Higher Self a chance to speak; so tiny is the voice at first, but as we gain confidence and it gets stronger, so we become aware of Beings that have trodden our path and can explain some of our deepest thoughts. We find this different experience interesting at first, but later a greater understanding and acceptance comes our way. We seem to 'bump' into people who are asking the same question, and are amazed to find one is not alone.

Where does this little voice come from? It is endeavouring to translate to us a world apart from life on this planet. An idea from other dimensions that can begin to unite the Beings that have graduated on this sphere. If we cast our minds back in history we see that gently and slowly things have changed bringing us greater conceptions of the growth on this planet, making us realise that it too has a voice, a life and experience of which we are part. We must investigate this and begin to help and bring forth the advancement of mankind, so that the philosophy of the 4th dimension comes into being and more and more souls can take part in the new thoughts, understanding them and initiating them to further enlargement. If this had not happened in the past, mankind would still be in 'caves', so what was that which changed things and made you what you are today?

To put it simply, one of those mansions the World Teacher referred to has been opened and another vista has shown its head. Like the world of Alice in Wonderland, a different picture has come on the screen – at first distorted and unreal, but later true reality has pushed its way through. More questions, more answers emerge and a flickering of a new discovery comes our way.

At this moment in time that picture is there on the horizon and it is showing itself to more and more Beings. It seems to be a similar picture to those who have reached that vibration. It is not a national picture it is a universal picture, and more and more can see/hear it. It is the Light from the Mind of the Creator, now itself so much more strong that it can penetrate the minds of men. It says the same thing – love one another, help one another and try and understand one another, at first through language and then through thought. Try to see yourselves as others see you and be ready to accept advice and criticism, and make a bond of realisation between Then and Now. You have elected to be here at this time of change to help that great universal power to penetrate mankind, and with the door of your new mansion just slightly open you can peep in and see the beauty of this New World or idea. Don't let it slip away. That door can so easily shut and it may take aeons of time to open again. If more of you who have experienced this voice begin to talk about it others will listen, more will get a glimmer of the picture and themselves get their mind on the course of Light and Love and seek further explanations of the reason as to why they were created in the first place, stimulating the 'Peace that Passeth All Understanding' and finding a pattern that must be the universal energy of the planet as a whole.

Each of you has to have a Purpose and Plan, so, therefore, must the planet, and as the power of the universe penetrates the planet so it, in turn, affects all life on it. You may call this evolution, but gradually each creation at its own rate will move into the 4th dimension. Note I have said 'At its own rate'; evolution is a slow process, it ebbs and flows like the waves of the ocean, but gradually makes its way in the new vista.

Science, the master of intelligence, has been exploring the physical Being and has made some great discoveries, but as the Age of Aquarius draws on it will bring forth discoveries and understanding of the mind – Jung touched on it and many are now seeking an explanation as to what it is. If the head of the man is opened up you will not find Mind. So, what is it? Where is it? Again, scientists, who must have understandable proof of their ideas, believe the brain is the computer that makes us tick. But what makes the brain behave as it does? Something very powerful, an energy that cannot be analysed, we call it Mind – that small speck of evolution that has come from the Universal Light. This is what mankind will question, explore and understand in the 21st Century.

Some Beings have touched on this and recognise the voice at the top of the head. They feel it has a connection with something else, and begin to battle with the idea that it is this Mind that makes the Brain tick. When that connection stops the Being is left unable to control the vehicle, and when that power completely withdraws you are, in your understanding, dead. But even then it must move on and live a further experience, as that energy can never die. All through the ages there have been men and women who have contacted and written about the 'little voice', and the only way most have been able to relate to it is by religion. This has helped to explain and translate what this power is; Master Teachers have given their ideas and interpretations from the various parts of the planet – hence different religions were born – but ultimately they all say the same. They must as the idea has come from the same source – know yourself, understand yourself and find yourself.

Accept and recognise that Mind is the first connection between you and ultimately the planetary force, and hence the Universal source. This makes you each one a part of the one force, all part of the greater whole. Does this not give you a more secure feeling that you are part of this planet and it, itself, is part of the Sun power that sends that energy which you call Mind? Now we come to the other question. Why do some Beings ask these questions and why are the questions very similar?

As each of you gets onto the same vibration, the same colour ray, it is inevitable that this should be so. This is the key to the idea that there must be a pattern, a realisation of some sort that initiates this thought. That thought, taken up by the Mind, moved into the brain, and ultimately into consciousness, is based on evolution. In your 3rd dimension form you base your findings on experiences. Having done a certain job for a while you learn and know how to do the work, but it often takes time and understanding to develop the way you finally finish the job. So if you move onto the 4th dimension it is logical to say the same thing is in operation, but you are using different material – a fabric that you can't see, hear or taste. Not to say it is not there, you have to learn the new language, the new experience, and hence we use colour and sound that is just as real, just as important as your materials in the 3rd dimension. So now let us look into this new dimension and see how it works.

Chapter 2

SEEING A RAINBOW

Colour is based on the rainbow as the white light sprays out into various fractions of it, each tiny spectacle giving off a colour as you see and understand it. The colour affects various aspects of life and is predominant in everything. Did you realise that you are a rainbow, gradually to relate to these colours by using and understanding the centres? These centres that stimulate your very Being, bringing in the energy to all parts of the body, are so important that when one or other of them is out of order it will be that part of your physical body that becomes dis-eased. So here is a language that needs to be investigated and understood. Just as the planet has its protection (ozone layer) so too has your body, and that is called the Etheric Body. It takes in the various energies, colour rays, from the sun and directs them to the various parts of your body, so you learn through meditation to accept and manipulate these colours. Some Beings can see them, others sense them, but you become more aware as you check on them. So you also are a rainbow and if you could see yourself on that level a very beautiful creation – just as the animals and flowers, etc. are in their own way.

As you identify with colour you will find it becomes stronger in various parts of the etheric body and you then relate to the appropriate part of the physical. Most beings, when asked, will tell you they feel the energy in the Solar Plexus – a highly emotional part of the body – and some will feel the colour strongly yellow. Others will feel more in the Heart area – green – and just as your physical heart has two sides (ventricles) so the colour green has two shades – grass green (yellow green) and turquoise (blue green).

You can see how your etheric rainbow is gradually changing and the cause of this is your experience and understanding of life. You start to think differently and hence bring to yourself a different realisation of who and what you are. Colour and its influence on the body moves to the Throat (blue) and one starts to use the influence of language much more on religious and spiritual matters and ideas. You are individualising so much and using the freewill that was given to Homo sapiens, opening up one of those mansions we have spoken about, and seeing and understanding a greater realisation of the world as a whole.

Nobody can train you to do these things, you have to do it yourself. You read it in books but it will mean nothing until you have hit the Throat ray (blue), and then you start to understand a little of the Will of the Creator – how it fits in with mankind – and you move on at your own pace. You sense pressure on your forehead, sometimes quite painful, and as you sit quietly you feel and see the colour indigo – very beautiful. A flash at first, and the more you accept and relate to it the stronger it becomes. This is the third eye that is being activated. 'The eyes are the window of the soul' is often quoted but this is incorrect as it is the eye that is the window of the soul. That part of you is now also beginning to wake up and, although it has always been there, you have not been aware of it.

This is the language of the 4th dimension that has been mentioned and one that you will eventually relate to as easily as you do the 3rd. It makes you address yourself and others in a different way – dare I say in light – and as you open to the different colours they, in turn, bring in different sounds, and you learn to play your violin and produce a beautiful sound that is part of the orchestra of the Creator of mankind.

When you have mastered and understood, and indeed accepted, the indigo vibration you begin to sense a disturbance on the top of your head – a pressure maybe. But as this gets stronger you are aware of a small voice, very faint at first, that seems to answer your questions. This is opening up the lilac ray and the vibration that the Masters can work on. These are

Beings that have trodden your earthly path and are able to advance a little further on the Path. They will choose you and not the other way round. You have to have reached this vibration before they can connect anyway. How do you do this? Through meditation and evolution.

It is through evolution – physically, mentally and spiritually – that we develop and control our Being. It is easier for you to understand the physical as that you can see has happened through millions of years; so why not mentally and spiritually? As your soul incarnates many times it uses the experience of lives to develop, and learns to understand and manipulate the brain in various ways. This creates different forms of intelligence, as you understand it, and helps to progress Homo sapiens. Why have some Beings so much more sense and understanding than others? You see people with similar problems: one deals with it and passes on, whilst the others cannot cope with it. Surely this is to do with experience in previous lives? The soul recognises the problem from before and knows how to deal with it, so the Being has moved on a little. This we call evolution – learning from experience physically, and now mentally.

When you truly accept this your mind now wishes to explore and understand the spiritual, and the pattern is similar; you ask where the ability to run, jump, see, hear and think comes from? What has given me the ideas and ability to read, write and consciously speak? And so we turn to the energy that has caused all this to happen.

To start with your Planatery Logos: it controls this Earth, getting its energy from the Sun; this power is condensed until it brings into creation the animal, vegetable and mineral worlds and yourselves; each form of creation gets a little more of the Planetary power and so other kingdoms are born. As that spark becomes stronger Homo sapiens develops intelligence, and that, in itself, will start to answer these questions. Hence religion is born and seems to be the only explanation. You seek to find a reason for all of this, and maybe religion is the only way mankind at that stage of evolution can give itself a reasonable answer. The Beings who have trodden this path realised that order and discipline must be implemented, and so rituals in their various forms were introduced. Homo sapiens have to worship something; today it is themselves, but many also see the need to develop a wider philosophy and develop an understanding of the God within – not without as has hereto been the order of the day.

As I have mentioned before in the past, the World's Teachers accepted and related to the vibration and understanding that was necessary in their area – hence the religions of Judaism, Christianity and Islam were brought forth, all believing in one creator, the Planetary Logos, but using different names and expressions that they themselves observed and understood. Each of these religions came from Abraham, and as you read and understand them they have much in common, but those who have not the evolution to accept and understand have made their rules and ideas appear to be the Real Truth. Many have gone along with this, but as mentioned before, there are always those who trod the path before and learned and remembered. These are the World Servers who are developing and opening that new mansion and seeing and observing, and some understanding, this new vista of the Aquarian Age.

I wish to try and relate to the 4th dimension – a dimension as clear and strong as the 3rd – based on colour and sound which are the vibrations that develop this. When the Being can touch the Blue Ray, it then asks these questions, and through intuition and observation (very important), it begins to pluck another string of that Spiritual Violin. Ritual, as such, will eventually disappear and mankind will move along the road where the individual has to make its own mind up and not be directed by ritual of any kind. Having passed through the religious incarnations, man now moves on to the Spiritual. It seems as if the great cathedral that he has been building can now have its scaffolding taken away as it is your own creation, strong and secure. One thing that is important is that you don't take the scaffolding away before the building is finished, or your Church/ Mosque will collapse and you are left with a need to start again and rejoin the religion from where you have come.

The need for religion is essential to the average Being; they feel secure and that is necessary for the soul of that Being. It takes time and many lives and evolution to start to look into this new mansion and realise you are part of that planetary Logos, and have taken that little bit more of the Energy that is there for you when and if you are ready. What is the purpose of this you may ask? Why did Homo sapiens change and develop into what you are today? Because some gradually touched the soul/mind that opened up the brain to a further realisation of the then 3rd dimension.

It is all relative. All the various roads/vibrations take their time, nothing can be hurried. If it is, and sometimes Beings try to develop a teaching that is not for them but maybe their friend encourages them, this can lead to great mental and physical discomfort. So, perhaps as you accept and understand the need for religions, and are ready to enter into a further philosophy of the Spiritual realisation, you leave this great house or temple with love and understanding to venture into a further dimension. Again this has a similar pattern but has to be geared to colour and not to the Church/Mosque responses that you have been used to. It also makes you completely able to accept the other forms of ritual with love and understanding – no feeling of animosity

Chapter 3

THE OTHER SIDE OF THE RAINBOW

Now the key to Spiritual Philosophy is meditation. In a way you have been doing this externally in your Churches/Mosques, but now it is internal, in the silence of your own Being. Here, once again, you need help from those who are just that little way further on the Path, as you did with your religion, and as always you will get that feeling, sending out an antenna that will find the group or person that can help.

Meditation takes many forms, practical at first and then as the mind stills and gets stronger and deeper, realisation occurs and you will begin to sense and hear a tiny voice – faint and distant – a sensation at the top of the head makes you aware of this. You have come a long way from your original self; still a long way to go, but you will 'bump' into those who are also on this Path and that gives you encouragement. You will feel very alone as most people will not understand, and here it is better to wait and talk to those who do. When the great revelation comes, and you are aware of this, then your Teacher will appear – he cannot reach you until you have reached this point, but he has watched you and hoped that one day it will all come into fruition.

This is the speaking in tongues that you have knowledge of, and you will find yourself talking with people about spiritual ideas that does not seem to be of yourself. Teachers have to wait many years and many lives, so maybe They can say in a humble way ' This is My Beloved Son in Whom I am Well Pleased', when the Being is able to be of use to the Master. Meditation, as such, has various degrees of development just like everything else; there can be a complete overshadowing by the Teacher, you may associate this with deep trance, where the Teacher is learning Himself how to connect with your Higher Self, and this can take a while as both Beings have to work together and be sure that this material that comes through is entirely that of the Teacher. Many sensitives stay this way as they are only able to achieve this kind of control, and many hold on to it and do not move on to the next stage.

The Being then becomes more aware of the voice – he can think that it is he who is speaking. The trance state is lightened and this is a more difficult stage to cope with. Again the sensitive will wait awhile, and when the Teacher is ready the Being will find himself talking in his own right, but of course he knows that the Master has control of the material that comes through. This is Inspiration – the true giver of Tongues – a great partnership between two dimensions, the one keeping itself well, fit and able and the master pleased that He has one more pupil ready to move out into the 4th dimensional world, and hopefully one day be responsible for training and teaching others.

I'm sure you have heard so many people relating how they heard or had an idea so strong that they composed music, or wrote a poem or a book. They usually accept there was a force behind this even if they think it is all their own work. Where do these ideas come from? Perhaps by reading this account you will get the answer. Everything must come from a central force; call this any name you like – Jesus called it God, Mohammed Allah – that direction that makes a man realise and understand that evolution comes from ideas, and those ideas come from the Planetary Logos, passed from one dimension to another until they arrive at the concrete state. If you have ever played the party game of Whispering, where a sentence is started and passed from one to another, as it emerges at the last person what was said at the beginning is often slightly or greatly different. So as the thought/idea comes from one dimension to another it depends on the quality and experience of the Being as to how it is received, and so as you open up this 4th dimension it takes time and experience to get it right from the Teacher. This bringing down to consciousness is so difficult and even on mundane instructions mistakes are made.

How often do you feel that you want to do something but the idea is pushed aside with some excuse, and either it is not done or a different interpretation is forthcoming to suit the easy way out – persecution or crucifixion, which of the two do we choose? Things enter our heads and our minds and we cannot conceive or understand why. But this is how to develop and learn the new teaching that must come our way, and eventually to all people. It makes us see it is necessary to understand ourselves, and begin to see once more why the Teachers looked on life in a different way from ourselves. People are not right or wrong in their interpretation of life, they are different. And that difference comes about with the experience of many lives and many cultures.

As we touch the 4th dimension our wants are different; in fact they become less and less material as we consciously realise that the greatest satisfaction comes from within, a contentment of ourselves that is far greater than owning a house/car etc. It is something that can only be experienced by yourself; and then comes the next stage of your crucifixion – are you going to take this Spiritual road to Damscus or are you going to stay with your material possessions and some of the friends that you have made on the 3rd dimension? Contentment is the prize and you will hear so many say 'Just what am I doing? Where am I going? All that I have is not bringing me contentment'. Like the musician or poet who has to write a song or overture, you too have to get on that road that keeps niggling at you.

The Aquarian Age is the age of the Mind, and it is shown as a Being carrying a pitcher. But that pitcher is filled with spiritual water that gradually overflows and humanity begins to feel the necessity to drink from it. Some of you have already tasted that water and crave for a longer drink, and as you understand this new revelation you will be able to partake of it as and when you like.

This planet is moving into another era – from Pisces to Aquarius – and this, in itself, will upset the whole planet. A New Age brings new ideas and energies from the Sun and that is delivered and taken up by the Planetary Logos and so eventually to humanity itself. The pattern is the same; you have to see where you fit in and try and understand that many who have not begun to see the overall picture are, in some ways, at a greater disadvantage. So perhaps you can understand why the world at the moment is very upset and unhappy. Beings all over the planet are affected by this new vibration and it affects them in different ways. The 3rd dimensional people mostly become aggressive and try to hold on to what has been, and equally, others wish to dispense with the old world but really are not able to see the good or the use of the past, most trying to run before they can walk and altogether creating a rather unhappy muddle. But those who have touched the 4th dimension and sipped from the jug are more cautious, ready to look into the pros and cons and try to see where the new views and ideas are going. A very disturbing time for these souls as they are not sure where these ideas have come from and whether it is right to concentrate on them. They find few people to discuss it with and feel very alone and out in the cold.

Then there are those who have started to tread the path and are quite sure where they are getting this definite instruction from. They migrate to groups or societies that are on the same wavelength, the same colour ray, and meet up with those who are further ahead and can help and explain things for them. They need the quiet, and through the meditation begin to feel the gentle ray of the Aquarian Age.

Again it takes aeons of time to develop a true understanding, but the more they accept the power of thought and the idea that all the power descends on them in various quantities, so it will take 2,000 years to achieve the new Teaching. Mankind will be very different at the end, not only physically, as that is affected by the new ray, but of course mentally and spiritually. Look at the history of the Piscean Age and trace that back to the start. How did man look and think then and at the end of the Age? See him now, quite different in so many ways.

Chapter 4

NEW CONCEPTION OF LIFE

My reason for writing this account is to try and put it simply and show you where you fit in, and when you have found your niche perhaps see where the next step is for you. I have felt there is not so much for the Being who is just starting to ask Why, Where How? It needs to be a simple answer in a language that is understandable, hopefully just putting out a hand to lift you over the stile and open up a new vista of ideas – colour and sound – that is just beginning to penetrate the mind and hence open up that new mansion in the brain. Many may read this with no effect, that is right for them and you should realise the reason. But some will begin to say that is how I feel, my thoughts then can't just be imagination, and now I have found others who sense and feel the same thing. This gives the Being a little hope and explanation of the whole concept of how Beings move through the 4th dimension and, of course onto other equally important dimensions.

There is a plan for the Planet – there must be or everything would be chaos. As the flower dies only to return the next year to produce itself, so the Beings on this Planet do the same, and indeed right through the solar system and the universe itself. This could, perhaps, come into the theory of Reincarnation – returning many times to learn just that little bit more, a greater understanding of the thing as a whole. Such difficulties in families are connected to this, and the odd one sometimes in the family will move off on its own to search for new explanations which the family do not want or really are not ready for. In your Holy Book there is reference to the Prodigal Son – at first understood as a story but, like so many myths and stories, there is a deeper meaning, all there for those who have eyes and ears to see and hear. But that story reveals itself as the Being opens up that new mansion and sees the true reason for relating it. Each of you, sooner or later, wants to leave home. You see this happening around every day; you feel smothered by the family and environment, so when it becomes strong off you go and all sorts of adventures await you – some good some not so good. You enjoy yourself with the new people and a different lifestyle. This can go on for a number of lives but sooner or later, just as you had that great feeling to get away from home, you begin to ask, where is this leading? Are you happy and content with your lifestyle? And you begin to feel life was better when you were at home, so off you go back to where you came from. A great welcome is awaiting you there, as you are bringing back experience of life and dropping it into the pool of a new realisation.

Your Teacher Jesus would say 'This is my beloved Son in whom I am well pleased' – helping to develop that central force that you call home to maintain a further dimension and eventually affect some Beings who, in the past, affected you although then you did not understand it. The Prodigal Son gives the whole message of development and growth, but it takes a while to understand and it is not until you are ready that this can happen, and then you say 'Why did I not see that?'. And so one may ask 'Why do you not see and accept the 4th dimension?' But, of course, eventually you will, you have to, evolution tells you so.

Perhaps as you begin to see the pattern and Plan of things life itself is not such a mystery. Invention of ideas develops into concrete reality, and so inevitably an aeroplane, a book, a piece of music comes into fulfilment. As the vibration of your Being changes so it, in itself, will enter into a different sound/colour Ray. Within that Ray there is much to understand and deal with, and like the story of the Prodigal Son when you have experienced and understood what that is all about, you will be ready to move on to the next Ray. You can help your physical body to move onto these

Rays by at first being careful about what you eat, and the idea of vegetarianism will enter your mind, You will feel the need for less food and a need to fulfil your hunger in quiet, gentle areas. Man has moved on to this way through many lives, gaining entrance to, once more, a different garden, a different perception, a different reality.

Much time is being spent in trying to discover how the universe started. It would be of so much more use to mankind if attention would be directed to how man himself is developing, the how and why of it, finding out and accepting that the key to it all is energy; that energy attracts and rejects vibrations, which are attached to the colour ray of the rainbow, which, in itself, is pure light. Each one of you is a part of the pure light, and dependent on how the energy is attracted or rejected, produces a formation of matter which you call animal, vegetable or mineral. But this exploring and searching is not of great use to you as a Being. What is of use is the necessity to find out who you are and why you are here. I do believe that many more Beings are ready to move on and become 4th dimensional Beings; you have the intelligence and understanding to do this if only more would devote their time to self realisation and the understanding of the mind in relation to the brain. This as I've mentioned before, is a computer and you see now how they work in the commercial world, then why not in the brain?

Any computer has to have an operator, so why not the brain? That operator is the mind and depending on the quality of the mind/brain, or the energy it evokes, so various results are forthcoming. In your holy book you are told you have been given freewill, something the animal, vegetable and mineral worlds have not, and that means you have that extra energy that enables you to open up a further part of the brain, and hence new vistas and ideas emerge. But this is something that comes from a universal energy which we could call spirit if you like. It is the essence of all life and understanding, and it is there to be tapped, and, could I say, watered down until it is able to contact that tiny part of you you choose to call the soul. So, the soul directs the mind and the mind directs the brain – hence body, mind and soul, so often referred to.

You have been given the freewill to investigate this, and this intelligence is something the other kingdoms have not got. So you are changing in your physical, mental and spiritual approach, while the others stay as they are. So let us try to investigate and develop this new you and see where it will take you and why evolution is necessary, indeed inevitable.

As you observe Homo sapiens you notice how different each Being is in all aspects of its creation, so why is this and what makes a sinner or a saint? As you tread the Path so many times gradually you begin to recognise the way and know how to climb the mountain without falling and making difficulties and mistakes. So you see some Beings are a little further up the mountain and others are just beginning to climb it. You yourself become more observant, indeed this is the first sign of the need to start to climb the mountain. Many do not notice the beauty and the sound of life, they are busy with their own life and maybe those around them – family – but, as I have said before, you ask Why is this? What makes the difference? And Where is the need? Then the mountain is there and you are ready to climb. The human race is beginning to climb more and more; Beings are watching and observing and feel the necessity to follow the others. Many get started but fail to continue – they are reluctant to give up on their 3rd dimensional attitude to life , and mundane things are too strong for them. But others feel the need to explore various spiritual philosophies and try to understand why men before them have asked these questions. The answers are in books but you have to find them, and indeed find the book that answers your questions. Like religion, you need a start: you have to find groups or societies that are investigating these ideas and you will move from one to another trying to find that which is necessary for you. This all takes time, could be a lifetime, but what is time? Something man has devised to suit his own necessities.

When the soul begins to make an impression on the mind, sufficiently to influence the brain and bring this direction into consciousness, you will begin to feel a satisfaction and contentment that helps you to answer many mundane questions. These answers are only necessary for you. Each Being is different, but at least you find there are others who are investigating the same ideas and coming up with similar answers. All the time you will be helped on your journey in this new dimension, rejecting and accepting as you move up the mountain. You may ask Why is all this necessary? Why has it been necessary for mankind to move from caves to houses, from horses to tractors? And for the need to develop a language that can be written down and passed on to forthcoming Homo sapiens?

You have taken all this as inevitable, but I hope you can see it has taken a very long time to get where you are today. And, again, if you look at your Planet Earth the development of its people is still at very varied stages of understanding, but I'm sure you can see there is equally a need to go on and find out more, this time about you as a Being. The need is necessary for the Planet as a whole as it is, in itself, a Being and it needs you as much as you need it.

Once you can see that all this is relative, the Planet develops and progresses as your own Solar System does, then you realise this is some sort of Plan – unknown of course to you and yet you feel that little bit of it; this is where the Mind comes in. It alone can feel or connect with the soul and eventually, with practice, can contact or influence the brain, and that is the organ that gives you the ability to bring to consciousness these ideas/thoughts that sometimes seem so strange and often not understandable – all taken for granted at first but, like any scientist, you can begin to ask how and why?

When these questions get into your consciousness you are entering another dimension, another understanding about yourself and the Universe, and maybe I could call this intelligence. It is this 'inter-telly' communication which your Being has got as you've opened up another mansion, and you are beginning to explore this different world of colour and sound. Why do so many mystics take themselves off to remote or quiet places and spend time in contemplation and meditation? Because in a way they have to. This is the path of Evolution and there is no way of stopping it. And, again, if you read and learn about these more advanced Beings who have trodden the same path as you but a while back, they have asked the same question 'Why?' which has led them on to a different concept of life on the planet, and a necessity to ponder and explore this new dimension.

One of the things you will note, they all have similar ideas and express them in sound meditation. Why do they all come to this conclusion? Because as they have moved through the rainbow and expressed and experienced the colour power of the centres, they have reached the head – lilac colour – and that in itself takes them eventually to sound. This, as the colour spectrum, takes different vibrations and will affect different parts of the body – you mostly will feel it in the solar plexus, but gradually, as you move on with life experiences and observations, you will feel it in the area you call the heart. Much misunderstanding has developed here as Beings connect the heart with love and kindness, but the organ itself is just a necessary part of the physical body. It is the heart centre/chakrah, that 4th dimensional part of you, that is pointing to the power in that part of the body. Feel it as a vibration, as in the solar plexus, so that sound power moves through the etheric body and you experience it as physical. But it is that very important protective body, the etheric, that makes you aware of a power in different parts of the physical body.

As you feel this sound you will feel vibration in the different areas – throat, third eye and finally head – and you have a feeling, coming of course from the mind, to make the sound that is necessary. A planetary sound used for all this is OM, the opening O and closing M of this power that you are now identifying with, and it is necessary for you to find your own sound and your own position in the etheric body.

Once you become aware of this and accept it, that is the important thing nobody can make you, it is a journey you make yourself and one you cannot stop because your intelligence and evolution has demanded it – you will have no doubt that it is there. Here you may find help and explanation from a society that you find right for you. That, in itself, takes time to find and you will touch many that are right for you for a while, but, like the Prodigal Son, you will need to go on your way feeling that inner and yet outer need to experience and explore new dimensions.

This is really the message of the 21st century where so many minds are equipped with the ability to ask such questions and decide where man is and where he is going. It is deep in the feeling and, to a degree, in the knowing of the Being who has reached this form of realisation. These are the spearheads of this Enlightenment, the Servers of Humanity where thought power or ideas stem from – many philosophers have in their time stated extraordinary thoughts, and many years later those ideas are found to be what the new philosopher builds his ideas on and extends them. If you think about it, where did they get these theories? Like you, at that time they were ready to catch or tune into the thought power which is always there and bring it into consciousness – just as many of you are doing today with the aid of language, books, reading etc. This is now developing so much quicker. More Beings are able to find out and ask and bring their thoughts to some sort of conclusion; once more man can move on and begin to form a new Race, new Beings with eventually a different concept of life from what you know today. This, of course, will take centuries, but must start somewhere, just as everything that you can think of has a beginning, whether practical or spiritual.

Chapter 5

A NEW AGE DEVELOPING

At the moment the world, or maybe the Western world, is tearing around not knowing where it is going. Many are unhappy physically and mentally, and some are already saying 'Stop, there must be something better than this'. Their whole Being has had enough and in spite of all the wonderful aids that are in vogue today, they feel they must search for something else, and gradually as they slow down and become quieter in themselves and give the mind a chance to communicate with the brain, they realise they are searching for an inner 'Peace that passeth all understanding'. As I have mentioned so many times, this is inevitable as evolution must take its place in the development of the mind/brain. Can you see a pattern emerging, a Plan perhaps, that seems to repeat itself through mankind – the rise and fall of civilisations? The same pattern is there, a need to advance and explore and develop some new ideas; or sciences that reach a climax and then descend into obscurity. But during this experience there are the few who have learned, observed and noted for use in their next incarnation. Try to learn some practical things and maybe in your next life you will be the Being that discovers that thought which you've accepted and developed in this life.

Where do the scientists, musicians and writers get their ideas from? Could this not be the answer? Most will tell you that it just came and they wrote it down, all in a casual easy way. Many do not accept where it really has come from, but you on the 4th dimensional vibration know. The one thing, of course, that has to be is that in the case of the Arts they must have the practical ability to write it down; and the same with the other aspects of the Arts.

With reference once more to the story that you know of the Prodigal Son, man takes the path of the mundane life at first, experiencing and enjoying all that that entails, taking responsibility in the form of seniority in a firm or government, often not doing too well, again until he knows how to handle that power with love and understanding, which takes many lives. I'm sure you can think of many who seem to just accept high office without much effort. They seem to know how to handle it and indeed they can because they have done it so many times before. Maybe this time they have got it right and so they are ready to move on to the next great experience – usually this comes in the form of religion. They feel there is something that must be accepted and that gives them, for a time, the explanation. It has its rules and doctrines that have been there for aeons of time, and it is a great satisfaction now, after many lives of struggling, to make rules and get them carried out, often at a great cost to themselves in health. They now have it all on a plate and they can enjoy and absorb this experience.

Religion, again, takes many lives working through to the Monastic order and feeling the communication with a greater force than yourself. But this is all really an outward expression, a ritual that is part of the teaching of whatever religion you have decided to experience – all have their rules, their dogmas passed down from generations of Beings that have directed, through language, what has to be. But here again eventually you will start to ask that great question 'Why am I doing this? Why is it necessary to follow these ideas that are all external?' And the mind again starts to have a stronger connection with the soul and starts to wish to express your own feelings of the wonder of life, as in the form of poetry, painting and music, each taking its turn to develop the brain through the mind.

Each expresses the 4th dimension in its different way: the writer through words, the poet through words and sounds, the artist through colour and the musician through sound, each moving gradually on along the road of discovery. All this is very necessary to understand and accept and be ready for the next signpost on this road to evolution.

The Arts, like Religion, take many incarnations to go through, all the time shedding and developing and building your own Cathedral. It has to stand strong, without scaffolding that I liken to Religion, as, whilst in these lives you have the great churches to protect and direct you, when you venture into the Arts you are building your own building based on what you have remembered and experienced in your previous lives.

Maybe, at first, the language of words, literature, is born – stories, mundane and spiritual, have your own mark on it. Taking its cue from the direction of the mind, getting its inspiration from the soul, as that taps the Universal Spirit, myths are delivered which, like the parables tell much when the outer case is removed. And so with poetry, in the same way, adding sound to the words and a feeling of the Universal rhythm.

Next, the colour of the world and its great beauty – you feel you must paint and express your feeling of this great Universal picture. Each sees all this in their individual way and develops it accordingly. You are using your eyes, indeed the 3rd eye, to express this. Hearing comes to the mind and beautiful music develops – you can hear the music of the spheres. All of this is there for everyone, but until you are ready and have the understanding and ability to see and hear, it naturally passes by.

When you have truly appreciated and understood the Arts, seeing where they fit into this great picture of the Universe, ask one more question 'Where has all this come from, am I making it up? Am I intellectualising this/have I read it/seen it/heard it? But what I have produced is not a copy of the past, it is coming from me as a Being, at last expressing my own ideas collected from aeons of time and evolution'. Then you move into the spiritual understanding of it all: how all this is necessary in order for you to develop and become a 4th dimensional Being using Religion, Art and understanding the Science and need of all this to become an integrated Homo sapiens, a Master in the making, a Teacher of mankind. You feel you are guided and yet must drive your own vehicle, but are humble enough to know where to get real help when necessary. The answer comes in the form of a tiny voice in the top of the head, very faint at first but gradually quite clear and strong; and now we come to the even more difficult part of making sure this is the real soul communication, not something that is just using your mind to develop its own greedy end.

So many have reached this point but have failed the last hurdle allowing ego and self-esteem to overshadow all this work. So often must you say ' Get thee behind me Satan' and truly acknowledge that there are forces around who, through your long journey, have tried to steer you away, showing you the material assets that could come to you and a beautiful picture of what could be. All through this journey you have to resist and reject and have many times made mistakes not recognising the wolf in sheep's clothing. But as you journey on hopefully you get stronger, and with the aid of that little voice – which only the few have earned and developed – you can make the decision that is right for you.

Here again I would like to point out that you can learn the ability of self-defence. Like any athlete, it is a training. Quite a simple one, but one that has to be remembered when you are unknowingly faced with spiritual danger – a strengthening of that most important part of your body, your etheric. Hidden, unseen but of vital importance to the Being as a whole. And how is this strengthened? Not by physical combat but by mind development, feeling the ability to use that force within, not without, to define and direct the way you as a Being must go

This unseen body is part of the Planetary composition and is, therefore, an energy that engulfs all Beings. It is that energy that provides and protects the physical body without which it could not exist. Just as you are hearing and learning more about the force that surrounds your planet, which is its etheric, so too you learn and feel and accept that this protection is there – rather like the sheath that protects the bud of a daffodil and very necessary to the flower. When you feel physically ill it is this etheric that has become weak in a certain area and forces, of a type that the body cannot accept or cope with, penetrate the physical. When you become more sensitive to this you are more able to repel those forces and so keep yourself fit and well; so once more you must investigate this idea and find how this is done.

Always along this road you will see the signpost that takes you to the person or group that is able to help you on this road. You will be directed towards meditation that helps you to quieten your mental and physical body, giving the etheric a chance to engulf your Being, strengthen the mind/soul and open up eventually that Higher Self and little voice that puts you onto the 4th dimensional road. Also, breathing has to be learned and understood. If you watch a very young baby that is in its purest state, you will see it breathing from its stomach. Check yourself and you will probably find you are breathing from your chest, sometimes quite fast. But the pace of the Being must slow down and develop that breath control that comes from the lower part of the abdomen – in through the nose and out through the mouth, in count to 4, hold and out to 4.

As you develop this you will begin to feel a power moving up to the throat and then you can add sound and the OM is introduced – again, in on the O and out on the M. All this takes time, but each Being arrives at the various states as experience and evolution is the key to all this work. Just as a musician hears the notes of his overture, so you hear the notes of the great void that is there for all to experience and bring to conscious level. Sound is vibration and vibration is energy, and this is the whole platform on which the development of all creatures works; from the smallest to the largest each able, according to their capacity, to open that 4th 'room' or area of the brain, that can bring the ideas and inspiration to conscious understanding.

An animal works on instinct, also Homo sapiens in its earlier stage of intelligence, but those who are moving on work on intuition – very difficult at first as it is often overshadowed by intelligence that has been used for debating and discussing and proving the 3rd degree of understanding. But as the Being becomes more sensitive it then gets to the knowing, as of course it is helped by that tiny voice the direct control from the soul that influences the mind to deliver to the brain. How often do you hear the expression 'I had a hunch'? Now whether you accept that instruction is up to your freewill and eventually to your faith – very difficult to explain to others but you become so certain that you cannot disregard it.

Those who have not reached this stage will not understand. Why should they? But you know, and better still, you know exactly what has happened in this work – it is really a matter essential to the development of the Planet and the Solar System. It is how it all began and how the Universe has expanded through aeons of time, all the while picking up that little bit of energy and using it to move on to the next great experience. At first I might call it an amoeba, that grows and expands and creates each extra bit of spirit life to formulate another design, another pattern to make yet another formation of matter. What are you but matter now made into a Being that has eyes, ears, mouth, all evolved through time? Quite inconceivable for you, maybe, to accept and understand, but as the senses developed and enabled this extra part to build up and produce Mind then Homo sapiens was away, as now it had some communication with the central force of life itself, and that developed the organ called the brain.

It opened up new areas the more it was used, and enabled man to speak and produce and understand language, and finally write it down – a great step forward as the children of the father can now read and do not have to each time keep working on their own experience. They now have the ideas and rules and laws that previous generations have learned through trial and error and they can build and go on from there.

All this I'm sure you are aware of, but what I am trying to do is give you another piece of the jigsaw, an understanding and a reason why you are, hopefully, feeling the need to look into and ask questions about this next mansion that I call the 4th dimension. It takes the same form and progression but, may I say, the language is different, and it is that language I am hoping to explain and develop into the New Age dictionary of acceptance. As with the 3rd dimension, you will have to devise, discuss and debate in your groups to learn and understand this new world; but each of you, as you accept and feel the realisation of what has gone before, will develop the energy and desire to move on up the great mountain of evolution.

Some of you are already experiencing colour: you may see it or sense it, and again in your education have already learned how it becomes and shows itself – hence the use of language and books that can be referred to and understood. So why now can you not realise that all creation is colour – tiny pieces of energy that spin off the great wheel of the lifeforce will build themselves into a tree, flower, creature, and you yourself are part of that energising force.

As time developed man tried to express this great idea and so had to make a name for it, just as the ancients made stone circles to try and explain the movement of the sun. It took a while before they got it right, but now you accept without question that the earth and planets move around their mother star the Sun. So you are trying to understand why colour, and ultimately sound, is intriguing to you. Once more you will get it wrong to start, but eventually the penny will drop and you receive that great new revelation. But some Homo sapiens have reached a stage where they can communicate with energies or Beings who can teach and guide them on to this new understanding.

When you go to University you have to have reached a certain stage in a subject; the professor is there to take you on to the next stage. I am hoping that as each of you has reached this stage, I can take you on to the 4th dimension and give you a realisation and need for this development. There are more Beings (than there ever was) at the moment just ready to enter the University of Life, and I and my fellow teachers must not let you pass by as it is essential for each and every one of you to move on to this new plane of experience. The Earth and the Sun, that give you life, need it. Beings need to transport the energy to those that are ready to feel, hear and see the New Age. One of the first indications of this Spiritual Energy is when the Being begins to ask the question Why and later Where? It keeps puzzling you and somehow there does not seem to be an answer.

Religion – there you are dealing with the outward and visible sign, and many make the Universal Power (call that how you will) responsible for the good and certainly the bad that is happening on this planet. Why does the great Creator allow all this suffering? But don't you see that it is your energies that have created this state of affairs? You have taken the route of passing responsibility onto somebody else – in this case the Universal teacher. If you had learned to listen to Him you, or your world, would not be as it is today. The modern idea puts the wrongs that are happening onto somebody else – 'It is not my fault, somebody told me to do this', etc. but you have to learn to stand straight and say 'No, this is not right. I feel, I know I cannot go along with this'.

Chapter 6

COLOUR RAY UNDERSTANDING

Many of you are now asking this question 'Why is this happening, surely there is an explanation?' Many are running away to the country to avoid these answers. For a while they will be happy but sooner or later that will not suffice and an inner realisation will creep in. As your soul, or Higher Self, gets stronger it begins to hear the voice and that moves to the Mind, and if it is still strong enough and has not been disregarded, will affect the brain that will bring it into consciousness. Now some Beings move into Religion which is essential on the journey, but here you are given the training and the answers on that level, and like the Prodigal Son again, must leave that direction and find out for yourself. Here you are now asking why it does not appear in any cult or religion? It appears through your own self, reaching up to the next vibration, the next colour ray, and there you will meet up with others that can discuss and encourage you to keep on the Path and learn the Purpose of mankind's reason for existence, and indeed the value of finding this different form of expression of the Universal Power.

I ask you to read and learn the Invocation and see how it moves from one stage to the next. Just as you learned the Lord's prayer, you will see that that keeps asking for help from above – an outward expression of your love and respect for the power you recognise. All very necessary, but as you move on to the Blue Ray you will need to find out the Plan and Purpose of all this, and this is when that question returns – Why? Maybe it is because you see the purpose of life on a different level, from a different viewpoint; all that you thought was important slides away and this other interpretation identifies itself. Like the escalator in a shop, as you move up on the stairs you can see the whole floor, where the different departments are, especially where the exits are; on the ground floor you have to find those places, but now on a higher level it is all quite clear. So you are moving up on this escalator and are about to find out more of the next level of understanding which is quite different from the ground floor. But still it too has its departments and exits – another part of the journey into interpreting the Purpose of Life and a further glimpse into the Plan.

I hope you will see these are logical conclusions as I know and understand on the 3rd dimension that is the manner and way you accept things; but, as I have mentioned before, the understanding is a little different. You are now looking within yourself, not being directed by religious laws but finding out what you yourself have gleaned so far on this very long journey through time. It begins to make you more understanding of others, as you see and hear things, and can really accept their difficulties. At the same time you are beginning to realise the reason certain things happen. Experience and Evolution is your answer, and all this comes gradually as you begin to ascend the escalator of Realisation and see the pattern that formulates as you move from plane to plane or from 3rd to 4th dimension.

The 21st century will be the establishing of the 4th dimension; so many Homo sapiens are ready for it. They have been asking the question Why, but don't seem to find a source that can give them an answer. Therefore my idea has been to put it as simply as possible, in a language that you can accept and understand, and hopefully will make you want to know more and be much more contented with your actual life. Money you have already realised does not bring you happiness or contentment and even those who have a lot of it get tired and begin to wonder what it is worth. But you yourself have to come to these conclusions and be certain that you have reached an inner realisation so that you become self-satisfied, content within yourself, and it is when you have reached this conclusion that you begin to ask 'Where do I get this other information? Am I alone or have there been others who have asked these questions?' Indeed, I would say man has been asking these questions all through the ages. It is thought-power that has developed the mind which, in turn, develops the brain, As you begin to tread your way 'back home' (Prodigal Son) you begin to understand the need for the journey in the first place. You have to explore and experience all things in order to understand the very essence of life itself, to make way for each new adventure that you are destined to take. As you develop this colour ray understanding, which is the language of the 4th dimension, you begin to feel where the power in your body is; most Homo sapiens on the 3rd dimension work from the Solar Plexus – the emotional part of your Being. But you will sense a movement to the Heart Centre as you drop the emotionalism and move on to the Green Ray. Like the heart which has 2 ventricles, this colour has 2 shades of green - the yellow green and moving on to the blue green.

As you sit quietly in contemplation you can check this: your breathing will slow up and you will begin to feel just where the power is, you start to slow down and feel the need for silence and peace. Some of you will feel that power in the throat, the Blue Ray, and then it will be very necessary for you to be in a group of say 2 or 3 fellow humans on the same colour ray. You feel great power if you get the right ones – 'When two or more are gathered in my name ...' I believe your religious teaching tells you.

On the planetary level you are connected with humanity, and the wide understanding necessary in that area – your thoughts, ideas and concept of civilisation – is noted by those of us who are listening and learning from our level about the great problems of the world that are at the moment causing actually so much disturbance. It is easier to tell someone what to do when you yourself are not part of that incarnation. Similarly, as the Heart Centre is connected with the Hierarchy (but you have got onto these rays by yourself and appreciate their necessity and the importance of what each ray holds), I am trying to show here that on our level we too have our sections of different understanding and, like you, have to tread our way (maybe in a different form or dimension) and move on from one plane to another. There are three centres of vibration or energy that we are concerned with and I have named them – Humanity, Hierarchy and Shamballa.

Chapter 7

MOVING UP THE ESCALATOR

Humanity (which speaks for itself); here you become attached to the developments of mankind, dedicated to helping your fellow Beings in various ways. This takes you into religion which takes many lives to work through and understand, and hopefully finally accept that all worship is the means to accepting the great power of the Universe; having a deep love and respect for God or Allah, and seeing that each has been the interpretation of some great Universal power – Poets write poems to IT, Artists paint IT, Musicians express IT, and spiritual philosophy knows IT – each section contributing to Humanity and trying, in one way or another, to reach with that energy a greater understanding and acceptance of each other, regardless of race or colour. The power is in the throat, telling the world of the need for a greater understanding on all levels, realising there is no right or wrong on a particular level – it is all according to the evolution of the person concerned. Many lives are spent dealing with the various sections of this – distribution of wealth, medicine, engineering, teaching and all, in their various degrees, have to be understood and used for the good of humanity and not for the good of oneself .

I'm sure in your history you can name many men and women who have dedicated their lives, and sometimes lost them, for those dreams. But out of it all each of you has to see the need for moving on to the next great centre where the Will of God is known. This, perhaps, helps to make it clearer that on each plane of realisation there are similar groups in formation that receive their instructions from a yet higher source of understanding. They, in their turn, have to digest and understand in order to pass it down to the next plane, and I, in turn, try to pass it on to you. I'm afraid in all these handing downs sometimes a little of the essence gets lost, and the most difficult of all is trying to communicate with the 3rd dimension as, with the form of education instilled in these Beings, it leaves little room for new teachings, plus the great problem of finding vehicles that are able to absorb and transmit them in a 4th dimensional way. But with time and evolution there are a few who have ears to learn and listen and hear the teachers of the next plane. So, what are they saying? In the quiet of your mind you will hear and know that this is all a continuous call from the Beings on the next dimension who are trying to help mankind to find a better understanding of the purpose of life. You are all trying to have a peaceful world but this only comes when you accept that each Being is at a different stage of evolution – regardless of class or colour. Those who feel the only way to achieve their goal is by bad propaganda or hate have to be understood, and a training of tolerance has to be put in operation; if needs be privileges taken away and a strict form of discipline imposed. If it can be explained to them that as they have not had so many experiences as others, and this is really why they are so aggressive, a picture painted to them as I have painted it here, maybe they will eventually realise and accept the provisional plan of things.

As the spiral of the planet turns in its own evolution it has to take a course of direction, and that, in itself, directs the course that it has to go. At the moment the earth has reached over half-way in its spiral, and so it is beginning to make its way back to, dare I say, the start. It is therefore inevitable that it will take in all that has gone before and, tinged with the experience of aeons of time, direct and integrate what it has learned. So what has to be overcome is man's emotion and aggression; with teaching and understanding of what I have tried to put to you, maybe you can make sense of the necessity to help it on its path 'home', and in doing so help yourselves. If you look at humanity during, say, the last hundred years I think you see that more tolerance has pushed its way through and more governments and people have understood and realised the need to talk and discuss, learnt to give and take, but of course once more this is where the wisdom comes in – that very rare commodity which only shows itself through experience and intelligence. Try to read and understand the history of the past, with all its faults which had to be in order that you could 'live' or evolve. Look at the depth of the reason for the difficulties and I think you will find most stem from the lack of understanding, and a desire to prove you are right at any price.

When you can come to terms with this teaching, based on experience and evolution, it gives you a feeling, I hope, of tranquillity within that stops the feeling of aggression and desire to be right at anybody's expense. So, as you enter the plane of the 4th dimension, the power of the solar plexus will rise, as I have mentioned before, to a different part of your Being. Silence and meditation is a must, your soul, or higher self, has to be given the chance to get a greater control of the mind and it can only do this in the 'Peace that Passeth all Understanding'. It will and it must, and like the planet you too have to get on your way since much is expected of you. It is impossible for me to explain to you how others are counting on you. It is how everything works in the first place – each little particle, so important to the next whether the atom or the Homo sapiens, and why we tell you that all is one, everything in its own way dependent on something else. Wouldn't it be lovely, as you move up the escalator, to look down on the 3rd dimension and see that experience as a whole; see what you could have done, but now realise you had not got going on that escalator.

If you have managed to stay with me and hopefully realise that each of you who is coming into the 4th dimension has achieved something on this long journey back to Reality, let us see how the 4th dimension will show itself. Beings will learn to experience colour and, in a relative way, see how that relates to the vibration of each form of colour ray. You will sense or see that this expression relates to different parts of the body and hence influences healing of same. It helps to make the understanding of the whole gamut of evolution – how this formation of the various vibrations which show themselves in colour, collectively returns to the Universal Light, that light that is the creation of this planet and ultimately the Universe as a whole. Colour shows itself in the various centres of the Being, and as it portrays itself in those centres it is a great power of healing. This will be the medicine of the future, identifying the area in the body that is dis-eased and directing that colour ray to the area in question. So, if you like, in the 3rd dimension you take medicine in pill or liquid form, in the 4th you take the colour.

Also, the method of diagnosing will be more accurate as you will be able to see the area in the body that is under stress – much as your acupuncturist today has learned that the pressure on the pulses is directed to the area that needs attention. So this means what you call the 3rd Eye will be developed, and with this observation it will enable you to see the cause of trouble. In one way the natives in the Amazon and the Bushmen in the Kalahari have still kept this idea; they do it automatically, but as I'm trying to show throughout this work, you have eventually to know why you are doing something so that the logic of the 3rd dimension, in one way, is continued.

If man has a greater knowledge of healing it will create a more sensitive Being and hence take him into a different attitude and understanding of life itself. As you observe a Being you will begin to see various colours moving in and out almost like breathing, because as your sensitivity increases you will see or sense that the etheric body is just colour. It is composed of minute particles that have yet to be discovered and understood. Because science cannot see this at the moment it does not accept that this very important body –the etheric- exists. Once it accepts this, big strides will take place in the understanding of the Homo sapiens. Take a pendulum and you can trace the power of the etheric body with it, and again, if you have the sensitivity, you can diagnose. With this it is just a confirmation that helps to prove to you the power that surrounds the physical body; add to this your new knowledge of the 4th dimension and see the colour rays permeating the etheric. Sometimes it is useful to give you the opportunity to have some practical proof and let you feel and see that a force exists.

Nature shows you these colours – look at the flowers and the different shades of green in the trees. Science has proved how this happens - part of the spectrum of light is missing and that reinforces the colour so you, as

Beings, are no different. All of this builds into a whole, the force of light, and that moves on to the next dimension which is sound.

Listen to a violin. As each note vibrates you can probably sense it in your top centre – a bell can give you this sensation and it makes you almost feel the sound. All of these vibrations and sensations are there for you to experience why you are in incarnation, and understand the purpose of the Plan of the Earth Planet itself. Many of you now are feeling these sensations as your sensitivity develops and you open up and use the various centres of your Being. You will develop this greater realisation and meet others who also have and are experiencing these sensations.

Chapter 8

HEARING AND BELIEVING

This planet has seven great stages of evolution to go through: it has now got past the half-way and hence my reference to the 4th stage that will allow it, like you, to further develop a greater power of the Universe and give it that extra ability to attract more power and hence express a broader understanding of its place in the Plan of things. This affects all life on the planet, and Homo sapiens, who has that extra thought power, will notice that something is happening. My idea, as I have said before, is to direct and help those of you who are asking the question Why? You have not found it in Religion, and often have not found a society or group that is satisfactory to you. Some have too many personality complexities and you just need to find yourself. So many of us have been like this in the past; always there are guidelines and Beings, in and out of incarnation, that have your answers. As we see the colour rays emerging from your etheric, we are so pleased to know one more little spark of God has shown the light and is ready to be helped along the next road of realisation. Up the escalator you are going, seeing a different vista and view of life and mankind, and this is how it is and how it will be – hopefully.

A few centuries from now this will be the norm in the development of Homo sapiens. You will be able to read your fellow man's thoughts and transmit ideas to each other via soul communication. Language, as such, will go as that is so limiting and can be misunderstood and wrong interpretations result. But when you can communicate via thought that is pure, a true picture can result. At the moment it may seem impossible, but look back on how mankind has developed from a Being unable to read or write to where you are today.

It is all necessary for the movement of life itself and the development of the Planet, and indeed the Solar System. This makes you realise that everything is so dependent on all forms of evolution, and why you read so often that all is one. Each little bit of life is there for a reason and is necessary. It is important to the progress of this Planet and why, as you have been given freewill and the great privilege of seeing and eventually entering that new room (as I have mentioned before), it makes you more responsible to all your fellow creatures – animal, vegetable and mineral.

This form of expression has not yet been given this further explanation, and to a degree lives on a day-to-day existence. A large number of Homo sapiens are still at the Atlantean stage of development – working on their Solar Plexus power centre and hence showing great emotion, but the Beings I am directing this thesis to, hopefully, have moved on to the power in the Heart centre which will give you a need for contemplation, and naturally control those emotions that have got you and the nation or world into such awful bloodshed. You can see this emerging in the statesmen getting together to discuss and trying to give and take and understand why things are wrong. All very difficult, and remember giving-in often shows strength not weakness – you have to be strong to take the backlash when you say 'Sorry, I was wrong'. Again, this needs to be used with wisdom as sometimes you have to give the opposite opinion. How much easier it would all have been if it could have been transmitted on a thought transmission; these mistakes and misunderstandings would not be there, but you see mankind can only learn this through evolution and experience. He has to get on the escalator to begin to understand there are different ways, and he himself must begin to change and realise that the whole etheric body must develop and accept greater forces of light that ultimately will develop and build a more integrated human being. Can you see how you are growing in wisdom and stature? How the power within influences your whole concept of life itself. You read

St Paul's experience on the way to Damascus. What happened? Nothing more than what I am trying to explain to you; he had reached a place on the escalator that suddenly gave him the great realisation, the direction as to what to do, because he was ready; and each of you, maybe to a lesser degree, is at that stage.

Some of you may have experienced a kind of revelation, some may have heard the sound of God/Allah, and you know there are other dimensions that you may not, at the moment, see or hear in the 3rd dimensional way. But that knowing is there and evolution will demand that you enquire into it and try to work it out – maybe by reading my simple analogy it will help give you that extra confidence to move on and feel the need to explore the 4th dimension. This great creation never ceases to give me wonder; all the time I, too, am finding out more and more, realising, like you, that there are far greater Beings than myself, not only on the Planet but in the Universe. Their source is Light, their power is Purpose and their understanding is God or the Universal Power itself. As you have had the privilege to read or write (maybe take it for granted) it does enable you to look back on History to see how Paganism moved to Religion. A slow development but you can trace it and, as you do, could you not ask yourself 'What Next?'.

The great teachers through the ages realised there must be one source, one power, and acknowledged that having lots of false idols only split the Universal Power, and that Power must be the whole essence of life itself. You have in your many incarnations been drawn to this Oneness, it then gave you an answer that was satisfactory to you at that time. It gave you an explanation and a security but now you are asking and looking for a further advancement on this question, and, as I have mentioned before, you have appreciated that religion has, as far as you are concerned, expired. You have built your church but it still has the scaffolding around it. Are you ready to take that down? If you do, will the church stand firm, or will it topple and fall? That will depend on how well you have built it. Now you are on your own, what will you do?

I hope you will begin to see that you are that church, you are the creation of the Universal Power, and as a Being you must now create your own religion within. We come to the words of many great teachers – 'Know Thyself'. Begin to explore Self-Realisation. Ask the questions about yourself: Who am I? What is Mind? Why must I find my own way 'Home' (Prodigal Son)? You will find many who are on the same path, you are not alone, and just as Paganism moved to Religion so Religion must now move to Spiritual Philosophy – that will be the Religion of the 21st century. This has no ritual, no class, no colour, it is an understanding of yourself, how your soul/higher mind/self eventually can direct the mind to control the brain to bring to consciousness the finer or higher influences of the power of the Universal Spirit which you often refer to as God. This will affect a small number of Beings at first, this is how your religion and the Muslim religion started, but with understanding and acceptance of that soul power they will see the need to move on to the 4th plane or universal realisation – a different view or different vista a little further up that escalator.

When you move into this new 'religion' of Spiritual Philosophy don't forget that many are still on their escalator, not so far up as you and indeed you have further to go; but remember to accept this and don't begin to preach or condemn as you were once there. You have had to learn tolerance of others and their views. It is easier for you now as you have an explanation of how, through evolution, one expression of creation must lead to the next, and now you have accepted that the Kingdom of God is within you – not without – what can you do for mankind? And not what you think mankind should do for you. It is natural that all Beings, who have reached a certain stage of development, feel the need to help those less able than themselves and, provided the voluntary work that you must do is from the heart and not from the need for self-aggrandisement, then you are moving forward on this great tide of self-realisation. One of the difficulties that seems to be showing itself very clearly is that of Health – many suffering from asthma and general breathing conditions. Much can be done on the physical, but more must be understood about the reasons for this. As the whole Being becomes more sensitive it requires different 'medicines' – meditation , silence, deep breathing and a general clearing of interference from outer influences. This is all very easy to say but so difficult to do. Here we come to the next great question – that of the Mind.

Scientists have done much to help the physical body and are beginning to devote more time to understanding the Mind. At first they are, in their 3rd dimensional way, tackling it on an academic level and so giving explanations and excuses as to the cause being environmental, family problems or educational misunderstandings. Of course these difficulties are not to be dismissed, but the real source is sensitivity caused by the evolution and development of the Mind/Soul. It is now taking on a greater grip and is demanding an acceptance of the 4th dimensional influences.

I hope you can see how all these complications emerge as you move up the escalator – it is inevitable is it not? So now you need different food, to a degree, to move you on your way; vegetarianism is one of the directions that will come to mind – at first the mundane reason cruelty to animals – but as you move through this you will appreciate that there is a little more to it. By taking into your body food that is of a lighter vibration and free, if you like, of animal cruelty, you will enable the Being itself to lighten and this will help to release the blockage in the Solar Plexus. This then, with the aid of a different understanding of and reason for your reincarnation, will help that Mind to bring forward a further enlightenment and so, sooner or later, a different Being is produced. By eating fruit and vegetables that in themselves are put there for you, no killing is necessary (they have been produced and are ready for the taking). Vegetables taken from the top of the soil are more sensitive than those beneath – turnips, potatoes, parsnips etc.– but as you understand and control your diet you will find that you need to eat less and, when you do, in silence.

Whilst eating you should be enjoying the richness of the fruits of the earth and, in a way, giving thanks for what has been provided for you. I see so many today eating and talking in noisy atmospheres but I must say this is no way for a now sensitive Being to conduct itself. Of course, as in all this philosophy you will come to this realisation yourself – you must – but I am trying to give you pointers that will help you to say Why must I be quiet? Why must I eat in a different way? Am I becoming, in the modern idiom, neurotic? If you are doing this because others are trying it and you want to be with them, then yes you are, but if you know you have to do this then all is well and you have the explanation in your Mind. Don't forget, as I have mentioned before, the Etheric body. That, in itself, is changing and so this will affect your physical body. Try to feel and sense it and keep it strong and clear of outside interference. I would suggest that you practise building up the power and, if you like, sensing that outer body; feel you are inside this egg-like power and that this very important power around your physical body is complete. Like everything, it is difficult at first, but as time goes by you will feel the need to do this when in a difficult situation and that protection will help save you from unnecessary stress.

Your scientists have now recognised that the planet has a protective field which they call the Ozone layer. It protects the Earth from a great deal of outer space interference, but like your own Etheric body, if it gets weak it is open to more of the Sun's radiation and space interference – materials that could have been stopped gaining access to the planet – and hence your Earth has to combat more alien influences than has been necessary. Your protective layer has been penetrated and disease of a different calibre has begun to show itself – may I here point to the Aids virus which is attacking Homo sapiens in body as well as brain? Can you see how the lack of protection of the planet affects your own Etheric body and that has permitted dis-ease to take place.

Now, as you have been taught, All is One; each little microcosm is as important to you on your planet all the time moving it forwards and back in its journey through the Universe. More is spoken of regarding viruses and you are finding that your present medicines are not standing up to them because they are in the atmosphere, difficult to identify and alien, in many cases, to this planet. Because you have tampered with outer space exploration, you have interfered with the Ozone layer and hence allowed the unnecessary interference to enter into the planet which, in turn, has and will affect all life on this planet. But those of you who are ready to accept this teaching will already be fortifying yourselves via the Etheric body and much of this will pass you by. As you are entering a new vibration, that of the 4th dimension, it will not affect you or your children as they will be schooled in this philosophy and also possess a more sensitive body which, through the Mind control, will fortify the brain and direct a different attitude to life itself.

Try to understand that the planet Earth is a living organism as you are. It must be respected, helped and loved as much as you wish to be. It can only give out what it has and, if you destroy that, part of it will be missing in you as you are destroying yourself. All of this understanding will enable you as a Being to make a better world and ultimately a better Homo sapiens. You need Fire (energy), Air, Water and Earth (food) in order to maintain your physical body, all part of the planet itself protected by its Etheric. Now just as you will have the understanding of the Universal Power, accepted and understood according to your evolution, so you are responsible to the animal, vegetable and mineral worlds. They too play their part and need your help, respect and love to give them a form of understanding – different of course from yours but in some ways relative to the same situation. Remember it is through them that you are here; they have evolved and helped the planet earth to make way for Homo sapiens, and you owe them that regard and appreciation. This all goes into the Teaching that All is One and, as I've mentioned before, everything is dependent on the other. You have moved on as you have opened an extra room in that mansion of life, and I have opened yet another room that gives me a different vista from my window of understanding. It is all relevant as we each move on in the light of our evolution; to see the world through the eye of a needle is, indeed, a profound statement, but sooner or later this must be.

I have spoken a little of the power centres of your Being of which there are seven. Now you will, with experience and acceptance of this, begin to sense and feel that power as they, in turn, open up like a flower gradually displaying one petal after another. It takes many lives before the whole flower emerges, but in nature itself you don't see a beautiful creation suddenly burst forth. Gradually you are opening up to the understanding of the power of thought which has always been there but, like so many things in your material life, they pass you by until one day you stop and see it all in a different way. As you move up the centres of your Being your colour ray changes and, as I have mentioned before, you display a predominating colour according to where you are. When you reach the Blue Ray (throat) we can see that tiny spark of light that, to us, is so precious and such a joy. Now one more of Earth's spiritual creation is ready to be planted in our Garden, very fragile and, like a tiny seed, sometimes does not grow; it is distracted by material life and false teaching and, in this life, may not show itself again. But never mind it will be there, hopefully in your next incarnation, this time to move straight into this evolutionary pattern. Can you see why some Beings whom you meet have a different understanding of life? Their attitude and comprehension takes an altogether different view. Maybe they were that little spark in their previous life and this time are showing themselves loud and clear to us; what joy to know that you are there and saying Here Lord, take me.

And so you move on to the Indigo vibration, the Third Eye (Ajna centre), and begin to feel the sense of oneness – more detached, more secure in your spiritual feeling – and here we are allowed to just drop a few thoughts and ideas that will help to touch that beautiful Indigo ray. With quiet and silence you will sense it in that centre of the forehead; it will fade in and out until you can control it and hold on to it. A great feeling of relaxation and compassion will enable you to feel the freedom of the Thought/Mind, at last it is getting through. You accept it is there, it has proved itself, and now you have hit the 4th Dimension.

This, of course, does not mean you discard your material 3rd dimensional life – that must be conducted and continued as it was. But this now is a little extra, it can give you relaxation and in so doing help to fortify your life in the material world. Today Homo sapiens is getting so tense, I believe they now call it stress, that it is upsetting your whole way of life. Everything seems to be moving at such a pace that you are finding it difficult to keep up; there is little quiet and in some ways, I'm sorry to say, this is done deliberately to keep you from moving up that escalator. Like most things, you have to be determined not to allow these material influences to get at you – the cause of so many breakdowns is that your higher self/soul is crying out to be listened to and your lower self is disobeying it. Can you see the conflict that is going on? Most of this comes about when your higher centres are opening up, the flower is half out and you must get the rest of the petals to open up; you are trying so hard but often just don't know how to help yourself, who to go to for help.

There are many around, some good some bad, who will give you excuses and maybe explanations, but all the time the teacher is within, just asking you to sit and be quiet and meditate and feel that centre in the head, only too pleased to help you on your way. You must surely see that all this is your life and experience and you must get there yourself. At this stage, as I've said, we can help a little but are so often rejected as you logicise and then we are pushed aside. My whole reason for getting this simple teaching through to you is to try and let you understand that almost the same rules are there in the 4th dimension, but as your colour ray changes you too will see or hear the sound of the Universe. How do you think the great teachers, poets, musicians, artists have achieved their works? They have got to this stage and, because of experience in a previous life, are able this time to put the idea into concrete expression. Most know that there is a something that gives them this power and idea, some still only accept that it is their work. But no matter, my idea is to give you a reason for all this and see why you have reached this situation and are not alone in your new concept of this spiritual understanding. So let us now move on from the Third Eye/Indigo Ray/Ajna and see what happens as we move on to the Head Centre.

The pattern must surely be similar but the ray is different, it is Lilac and this vibration opens up that little voice. You begin to sense and hear, and hence we are dealing with the Sound Ray; you will hear the voice very faint and gentle, and will wonder if you are making it up, but it will persist and give you confirmation that your idea or understanding is correct. Now I'd like to make an important point here to those who will, quite rightly, say this is what disturbs people and is exceedingly dangerous. If you check on the people who get possessed by this you will find that their voices will not come from the Head Centre but from the Chest Centre as if something has got into them. This must be cleared by a good healer who can deal with this, release it and send it on its way back to the stage of Evolution from whence it has come. But when you yourself have learned enlightenment and your top Centre is opened up, this is a God-given gift accepted and protected by the Hierarchy themselves. Feel the power there and listen to the silent voice – this then is your direct communication from thought to mind to brain. How often have you said 'I had a feeling about such and such' or 'I was of two minds as to what to do'? Here we have the battle, once again, between that pure thought and the instant logic of the lower mind – very difficult to understand and for you to accept. Just as you work your way through many lives through the Colour Rays – oh yes, they get into a muddle, but again with use and experience you will sort them out – so on the Sound Ray we have the seven notes of Wisdom. Music, the highest of the arts, has already accepted that they produce beautiful symphonies. Their Masters have accepted the sound and written it down. They have brought it to consciousness and you have the joy of their inspirational work so you now will hear the

Music of the Spheres and maybe next time will be able to produce a wonderful concerto.

This all comes naturally, must not be rushed, and where so many Beings go wrong and get hurt is to start doing exercises without supervision and trying to run before they can walk. Time is of the Homo sapiens making, ours is different so who is in the great hurry? On the 3rd dimension mankind is exhausting himself with speed and noise which is upsetting the physical and mental body. It should be a quiet, gentle process that, through directed and protected meditation, leads to the various stages that are necessary for you and you alone. A friend may have moved to the Third Eye vibration but you can only feel and deal with the Throat vibration. Don't try to compete. Very few Homo sapiens are on the Head Centre and they are usually being trained in Spiritual Philosophy – ready for the end of the 21st century.

The contribution you make is your thought transference – it works both ways, we all dip into the great pool of life but first you have to acknowledge that it is there. For many lives you have passed it by but now at last you see it and wonder what you have to do to know how to make use of it. 'Be still and you will hear God' they say, but what does that mean? You begin to feel an inner peace, it may not last for long but you feel there is something different – a beautiful tranquillity that 'Passeth all understanding'. Of course that is so. You cannot understand just what it is and for maybe a second you feel that calm which many today, in their stressful lives, are searching for; so they run away from the cities to the country in the hope of finding this Jewel in the Lotus. But until you have an inner realisation, and can begin to logicise in your normal manner again, you will not see or hear that beautiful pool of illumination. It can be found in a town or a country village because it is you who has to find yourself and then you dip into it and feel refreshed, give a sigh of relief, at last I am on my way Home (Prodigal Son) – a long journey that each of us has to take. Just as a child crawls, eventually it stands up; it has to fall over many times but sooner or later it finds it can walk. When we have seen that light and can contact it we receive great joy and satisfaction that one or more of our initiates is on their way. Hopefully this helps to make you feel you are never alone, there is a friend nearby with great love and compassion who will help by putting thoughts into your mind – but can you send them into consciousness?

There are signposts that point the way to this different understanding, put in the form of inner questions that make thought more provoking and bring you to a point of further investigation – What is the purpose of life? Why am I here? Is there life after death? What makes one Being so different from another? What or Who is God or Allah?

Many Homo sapiens just accept what life has dished out to them. They feel their own life is the only thing that matters, and accept the form of society they find themselves in. A few have an urge to better themselves and a very few are successful, but after that what? Some of the above questions begin to creep in, and often around this time you will meet or read about these very queries. Can you see Evolution shining up and giving you some of the answers? What is the purpose of life but to become a beautiful flower, a radiant person and someone who has found contentment and self-knowledge. Occasionally you meet such a person and you wonder why they are like that. Often their material possessions are few because they have already learned that you don't need a lot of these things – just sufficient to get you along in the 3rd dimension in which you find yourself. So, why are you here? To spot the necessities of life, a different approach, a greater acceptance of life as a whole. Have you noted the signpost or have you passed it by? Maybe not seen it at all or perhaps just aware that it was there. But eventually you will find that thought is still there and you feel you must go and have another look. A book, a person may be the answer to your questions, and that helps you to go along the path which will lead you to Enlightenment, that makes you into a different Being from your fellow Homo sapiens. Most of you are getting very concerned as to the planet Earth's situation. You feel you want to help, but in what way? Also, why is this happening?

Back to these questions. Now that you have, I hope, accepted that Evolution is the way that all things must go and that there is a Plan for all things, you can see that the Earth itself moves on a path and takes its course in a similar way to yourself. There has been a great mystery about the way water has flowed over the Planet, and reference is made in your Bible to the Flood. This has happened more than once because as the planet moves around your spirit-Sun it changes its position and creates, after a period of time, a tilt and this affects the landmass and creates a differ-ent formation or position of the continents. It helps to cleanse the planet, if you like, and hence different land masses appear and some disappear.

All of this takes its turn in the path of evolution. Much has already been found out and explored by your scientists and this, in turn, throws light on more of the mysteries of the planet. So, how about the mystery of your life? Can't that, in itself, be taking a turn in this pattern of evolution? You are a planet, a microcosm in a macrocosm and, to a degree, take a similar course. Your little spirit that is part of the spark of light of the Sun, which you can call God if you like, is giving you the power of life and understanding, and sending its energy through, enabling you to, as you call it, live. It holds the power and wisdom of this Solar System and, of course, there are many more systems that are doing similar work – some more advanced and some less.

How logical the Egyptians were to worship the Sun. They saw it as a provider, and isn't that what God is? Give a little thought and thanks to 'My Lord the Sun' and see yourself as a tiny spark of that Great Being. You have had your tilts through many lives, moving from one dimension to another, forwards and backwards, until you sustain yourself and are sure of where you are and where you are going. As I have mentioned a few times, I am trying to let you see and understand that there is a pattern and a Plan – as mentioned in the Great Invocation. As you read it a deeper un-derstanding will come your way – this is why you need to learn and say, or read and say, it like the Lord's Prayer which is another Mantram that holds great power if it is said with understanding and conviction, but so often it is gabbled through and becomes just a collection of words. Certain words have more power than others, but it is how the mind relates to the soul control that gives the Being God's Grace. Silence and contemplation is the key, not the noisy responses that rebound from your holy places.

As you enter the 4th dimension by this form of thought recognition, you influence your whole brain and so eventually change the DNA struc-ture of your body – your little Mini becomes a Rover, not yet may I say a Rolls Royce! Again you can achieve greater realisation, see greater vistas if you like, and once more, may I suggest, move further up the escalator. One of the greatest realisations that hits the concrete or lower mind is that now you need a philosophy that is Ingoing, an acceptance that your 'Peace

that Passeth all Understanding' is within, and you are finding out and realising that, unlike religion which is asking for help and what you want, you
are now seeing that you have to contribute and give of yourself – a draw-
ing in and expounding and not the other way round. The great musicians
like Handel and Mozart all heard the Music of the Spheres and brought
it down to consciousness; maybe you are not yet one of them but you are
on that road and, through saying the Invocation and the Lord's Prayer in
your own silent church which I mentioned you have built through many
lives, you can now enjoy and perhaps hear the sound.

Chapter 9

THE WAY TO GO

During my little talk to you I have touched on the development of the Spiritual side of Homo sapiens, how you learn through lives of experience to accept that you are indeed three in one – material, mental and spiritual. Could this point to your religious conception of Father, Son and Holy Ghost – all avenues that you have to explore on your way to the Holy City, whatever that may be in your own conception? Again I would point out how you have been taught, through many incarnations, to accept and carry out the ritual of the teachers at that time. In their wisdom they knew you were not ready to understand what they had conceived, so like all good teachers they tried to simplify, and hence myths and rituals were the result; still very much used and in existence today, but how many of you are on your way to try to understand what indeed has been happening? A greater conception of the whole idea is put in your mind and hopefully it is making it all seem to be so much clearer and acceptable, and your many questions are beginning to receive an answer. Of course they were there all the time but you were just not ready to understand and they passed you by.

In your Holy book you are told that God made man in his own image, hence some have painted Him as a Homo sapiens, but what they really mean is that the whole conception of the Being, made up of all the particles and properties of the Sun, eventually produces a Christ that is the Light of the World. You are part of the light which is gradually growing stronger and hence, to a certain degree, can absorb more and more of the understanding of the Plan. The Father, if you like, can now pass on to the Son a greater understanding of life – the Holy Grail. Are you ready to accept it and, if so, what are you going to do with it? All of this comes under the banner of Evolution, the call that eventually takes you onward into the 4th dimension, having observed and understood the 3rd, the Trinity, and ready for the next – the four aspects of Earth, Water, Air and Fire.

Now what kind of teaching would you devise to explain and simplify that? This now moves into the scientific field and that moves into the 5th dimension – Mathematics. So you see how symbolism creeps into this philosophy; the Triangle, the 3rd dimension explained as the Trinity and named the Father, Son and Holy Ghost (or Spirit) – the one reliant on the other and very necessary to each other. This is the whole outward interpretation of the Trinity. Many today do not really understand the purpose and the need for this symbol, but by now I hope you do. Also, whilst religion remains with its past teachings, it does not help the more evolved soul to get a grip on the Being and help it to move on to a further understanding and interpretation. You will no doubt question and debate this, you must because like a diver, you have to be aware of the waters you are going to confront, but dive you must and once more face another set of currents that will test and question your belief and faith in the story of Evolution.

What is this new symbol going to be? May I suggest the square? It takes the necessary dimensions in and holds the four elements in balance. You, as a Being, must begin to understand yourself – not only your beliefs but your physical self. Insufficient attention is given to how that poor old body, your home in this life, works. The more sensitive you become the more you feel the pain but, instead of taking pills, realise that through silence, relaxation and, dare I say, meditation, you can perhaps know yourself and indeed cure yourself; learning to refuel by deep breathing, coming from the stomach and not the chest, so that the flow of life-giving oxygen can get right into your body; not allowing yourself to get stressed but able to say to yourself 'Hold on, I will not allow this situation to influence or upset me', stand back from it and allow it to pass you by. Once your mind can get a grip on this it will enable and direct your soul/thought through to your brain and into consciousness. I am trying to explain and help each of you to understand how your whole Being works. Once you can accept this then you are really in charge and ready to truly drive the vehicle without a teacher or preacher at your side.

You can interpret God or Allah as you so wish – some of you feel or sense or see perhaps a Master that is like you but has gone a bit further along the road, and maybe has a more realistic way of helping you to paint your picture. But, as I have said before, when that little light or spark shows up in your Being you will be noticed and given help in the Mind as to the interpretation of Science or the Spiritual understanding of life. So many Beings feel alone, but if they would only allow themselves to stop analysing and just accept the beauty and joy then the grace of God will be there for them. There are books that have developed all this so much more, but I wanted to give a simple introduction and hopefully make you feel you want to know more.

The planet itself, like you, is ready for a great change. When man created fire and he developed machinery in all its forms it took mankind on to a further understanding and civilisations rose and fell, so that in the beginning of the 21st century a better understanding of the Mind will develop. Those who are ready will truly know how to use it and accept that it drives the brain; they will also realise that the essence of it all is thought – that is so delicate that it soon gets lost as it makes its way into consciousness. It is all relative, you are part of the planet and the planet is part of the Solar System , and the energy that is the creator is the Sun – could this be called perhaps Son of God? Why has this been portrayed in religion in the first place? One thing must lead onto the next on whatever level you think of – there is a Purpose and Plan and you are a vital part of it. Once you realise this it makes your life so much easier to understand. So many things that go wrong for you are the result of misunderstanding in a previous life and, in order for your Being to develop and advance, these handicaps have to be acknowledged and worked out – the name more often given for this is karma, and why, as mentioned in your holy book 'As you sow, so shall you reap' makes a certain amount of sense. I hope it helps when unpleasant experiences hit you. With some Beings this makes a scar that will always be there, but to others who have accepted and understood this teaching it is taken as an experience that, this time, must be put right, and grudges and hate must be eliminated. The Buddha says 'Put out the fires of hatred, greed and delusion': he is referring to your three lower centres and if you look at it these three expressions of Homo sapiens are the feelings that can ruin your present life – red, orange and yellow in the colour language which shows up so clearly in the aura of the Being. These colour rays will be seen and understood in the 21st century; instruments will be devised to help see this and hence doctors, who have accepted this teaching, will be able to diagnose and treat the Being so much better. The cause of so much violence is rooted in the three lower centres – something has happened in a previous life that is still festering away and needs to be lanced, treated and healed, not given excuses for. The Being has to take responsibility for why they have come to this state and 'Forgive those who trespass against us, lead us not into temptation'; in other words, see the thing for what it is, release the hatred and stand up to the delusion – that is the most difficult of the three. Hence, the Solar Plexus, the emotional centre, is where most Beings are stuck today.

Emotionalism has to go. It fans violence and leads to all sorts of dreadful things that will take many lives to put right. As you learn to feel your centres you will experience that pain in the stomach as if something has hit you. Note it and ask yourself did I put out that thought or did it come from somebody else? I'm sure, if you really think about it, you will get the answer. When you meet up with a truly understanding Being, you will find them compassionate but not emotional. To a degree this is what the psychiatrists are doing but often, because they themselves are not integrated Beings, advice is coloured by emotionalism – trying to so-call help the Being from really accepting it as their fault. How difficult it is to say sorry, especially to those nearest to you and vice versa.

It is often taken as weakness but if it is truly understood it is strength – to allow yourself to be laughed at, if you like, and not to take offence, this is a strong Being, and one who has no chip on his shoulder but can accept and understand why. Then you are moving away from 'being yellow', an expression I think that is sometimes used, into the next centre – the Heart.

Here we have come to the love centre. Which love? The love of self – yellow green, or the love of mankind – blue green, the one selfish the other selfless. Not unnaturally the Being becomes self-satisfied with itself, enjoying all the gains in wealth and happiness, doing so many interesting things which either make or break them, and hopefully learning through experience the joy of living. Why not? Maybe you've earned it, but are you learning from it? Eventually it dawns on you that you only need somewhere to sleep, something to eat and a healthy body. What was all that chasing around about? How long have you been doing it? Could be many lives. What was this wealth and happiness you craved for? You read about or meet up with a Being who seems to have so little but seems content and adjusted. What are they doing to become like this? Usually the answer is they are contributing to the world, have achieved a love of giving not taking, and that selfish love has turned to the giving of love - not emotionalism but selflessness - that is the beginning of the path to self-realisation, the start of the road home (Prodigal Son).

I hope as you read my story that you see where you are on this journey, and because you have taken the trouble to read as far as this it gives me great joy to know that that little light I've been waiting for for so long is now beginning to show itself. One of us will be noting, only noting, it and hoping that you are ready for the movement to the next Colour Ray - Blue. Can you see that as you move into another vibration or Colour Ray you are automatically touching other frequencies, and these in their turn will give a different realisation or understanding of your physical and mental body. I am interested how this affects you as a Being, but science would express it in another way. The throat area takes this colour and here we are, of course, using speech and sound. The quality of the voice is often shown in its expression of feeling; when the vibration has achieved its worth, it holds a soft gentle quality, and these characteristics are evident in the production of the sound. Now as these sound rays reverberate they are picked up by a group, if you like, of Beings who are working on this Colour Sound Ray - working for Humanity and the progress and development of the planet. This is the Being's first experience of contributing to the planet and putting its own little bit of experience back into the planet as a whole.

I mentioned before that it takes many lives before the realisation that gives the understanding that you have to give, not take, in this whole evolutionary system - many without thinking or understanding, are taking, often unknowingly most of the time. When you arrive at this centre you will have accepted this and your natural dedication will be on these lines. As we in the Hierarchy look for the spark of the light I mentioned, to pick you out of this great sea of evolution so, as you hit the colour blue and its vibration, you are noted. Just noted at first, and your power of thought that is now expressing itself as a Giver or a Server will be incorporated into this great spiritual field called Humanity. Maybe there is a reason why the Virgin Mary is portrayed in blue robes: her great love of Humanity produced one of the greatest teachers of the planet. So much of the spiritual teaching shows itself as you investigate and realise that there is a pattern and a Plan. How else could the world go round? This is my Purpose to try and relate spiritual philosophy to you as a Being, to let you see that everything from the smallest to the largest in size or Purpose is essential to the working and development of the planet – we could go on to the Purpose of the planet and to the Solar System but I hope from this analogy you can see the larger Plan.

It's an interesting journey and as that new mansion is opened up ('In my Father's house there are many mansions') so the vistas and scenery make a different impression on you as a Being – does all this help you to understand why it is necessary for you to have these experiences, and more importantly to understand why? Religion has taught acceptance, but like any child, after being taught to do this or that, it will come to a stage where it wants to know why and maybe all this will help to answer that question. So as you get a greater understanding of your mind, how it can help to direct and bring forward a conscious acceptance of how you and your Being relate to the greater wisdom of creation, so also the planet itself is making its way on a further realization of its place in this solar system. Man at the moment is trying to find out how the Universe started, where or how it was created; he will have to have a greater understanding of himself before that question is truly answered, but the fact that he is asking these questions gives a reason for his inquisitiveness which only a very few Beings are wanting to know. We come back once again to 'Man Know Thyself' and then much will fall into place.

More and more people are talking and enquiring into these questions so evolution is moving on and the great tide of experience is taking hold. Nothing can stop this, it is how man has developed from the beginning of time; just a little more light has penetrated into the Being and a new thought, a new idea has been born which eventually moves into consciousness. You may ask where has it come from? Your artists and musicians will give you the answer – they may paint it in a different way but the source of the answer is the same. Most will tell you they just had to express their feelings in words, paint, music – but the essence is the same, it is only the expression that is different.

Back to sound and colour once again which is expressing light in its whole conception, and on to the realization of a main force that is coming from somewhere. Each of you, as you reach this plane of understanding, is touching new worlds, new explorations not in the physical but in time itself. Your whole Being is moving into new worlds and you are so often saying 'I have only just realized that and it now is beginning to make sense.' And so you have to give yourself time to appreciate the beauty of the planet, feel the freshness of the wind, hear the music of the spheres, and have that inner peace that so many are searching for and don't realize it is there in front of them all the time.

Each of you is a Master, or God if you like, in the making; all are children of the Universal Mother, but each in a different form – some are infants, some at University. Each will acquire the ability to enter the University of Life, but the qualifications are different from the material University. Now an understanding is required in your ability to grasp the source of knowledge, not reading about it but to find out about it and accept that you have to acquire it yourself and not quote from what others have said, who, after all, were only a little ahead of you on this Path of Enlightenment. Shall we continue on the Path and find out what next?

I expect you have noticed I have been chasing the rainbow through the Centres of your being, relating them to colour and hence bringing in a different vibration each time, and so we move into the beautiful Indigo. Like the night sky it seems to hold a great mystery of some sort. Behind it or underneath it are the stars twinkling away and making you feel there is so much more than you; a greater something and maybe other Beings similar in thought to yourself. Hence, like this mysterious hidden feeling, you suddenly realize that you have now struck the Jewel in the Crown – the sight of your whole Being, the vision of the whole Purpose of this life.

In the East they show it on the forehead, and you also now are experiencing it as the Third Eye – the eye of illumination. You will just get a flash at first, but as you sit quietly it will fade in and out. It takes a while to hold it, sometimes a lifetime, but you will feel you want to stay with it as it is such a beautiful colour and feeling. A slight blink of the eyelid and it is gone, but as you acquire the spiritual knowledge and understanding it will keep coming back stronger and stronger each time. In meditation you have been learning to control your thoughts and ultimately to bring them to nothingness, but actually you really have been going towards this Jewel in the Lotus.

It has remained hidden and unattainable until you can touch that realization, and now it has, just for a second, let you see that it is there. Your glorious flower is now opening up and eventually will give you a deeper acceptance of this journey through the unknown to the known itself. Have patience, it will take time, but what is time? It is irrelevant, just used as a quantity to suit man in his present form and it varies even in your earthly experience as you use it in different ways – in happiness it is gone in a flash, in boredom it takes so long – but it is the same Time. Just like the Indigo, it is there for a second and then gone, but hopefully it returns as you yourself open up into the true realization of your incarnation.

So we move on to the next colour in our rainbow – Lilac. This will only show itself when the head centre is opened. For many it will take a number of lives before comprehending that you are in this life and need to communicate with your soul/spirit. Like the Indigo you will only be aware of it for a flash, but I have to say 'Only a few are called' and sooner or later you will be aware of that inner voice that gently speaks. It is so faint that you reject it, but it will persist if you have truly reached your Head centre. Here a word of warning must be given as there is a difference between hearing voices and listening to the word of the soul. This is your personal property if you like, and a reward for many lives of experience and wisdom, but voices are interference from other sources and usually are experienced in the chest area – as if something has got inside you. This must be dealt with immediately and needs the experience of an occultist to release it and send it on its way.

Now here we come to the most important part of the realization of Spiritual Philosophy – the knowing that you are in command of your

own Being, guiding and directing it through the knowledge and experience of your higher mind, accepting and realising that all power and
understanding comes through the energy of thought, having a true identification with your soul that is being brought into consciousness via the
brain. Through meditation, within the peace of this understanding, you
will know that a force/teacher is helping and guiding you.

As the Beings on this planet evolve a new form of Homo sapiens will
emerge – indeed there are a few already in incarnation, Beings who of
course are finding their incarnation very difficult as they are much misunderstood, alone, quiet, intelligent, having little time or interest in the usual
mundane form of conversation; indeed, Beings who to others have little to
say as they are already using thought communication which will cut out
a lot of misinterpretation of situations as they occur. Like the movement
of the colour rays, they are working on the Indigo and can see through a
situation, and indeed quickly analyse the problem that is in question. Their
answer will often upset the mundane Beings of society whose concept
of life is that they, like so many in the past, are difficult people. Look at
your history and you will see how those with different ideas were often
scorned, only to be proved right many years later.

Everything of course has to start somewhere and will always cause a
disagreement until more thought power on that idea is worked through.
As you are moving along this path are you one of them? Do you identify
yourself with this form of comprehension? Here you will indeed need to
find others of like mind to satisfy your feeling and understanding of this
new concept of the 4th dimension. As I have mentioned before, something will have to be substituted for religion; accepting evolution as the
kingpin, you can see how things in various directions change. As you get
more and more in unison with your soul/spirit this is inevitable, just as
the physical body is slowly slowly changing, so also is your understanding
and attitude to life itself.

My reason for directing this is to point out the Plan and Purpose
of this interesting and revealing journey back to its original conception.
Everything moves in a circle, but each circle moves on just a little bit and a
world of colour – sound – emerges. In your holy book it notes that 'God'
created the world by sound, noted there as the Word. If you drop a pebble
in a stream you will see the little waves moving around it, extending all

the time, and so the sound – depicted by some as the AUM - sends out vibrations that collect at various levels and create, each group identifying itself, in your language, as animal, vegetable or mineral; each part of the Tree of Life, with branches developing from the main centre, is essential to its wellbeing and development. This is just a picture to paint in your mind/brain to give some explanation of the wholeness of creation of which you are a part, why you are told that everything is One, so try to understand that as Homo sapiens you are part of that tree. This should make you realize that you are responsible for those lower branches and are there to protect and direct the growth, if you like, of that tree.

In the 'Garden of Eden' two trees are mentioned – the Tree of Knowledge and the Tree of Life – and again in the wisdom of that text direction is given to the Tree of Life. This means a grasp or understanding that only many lives and evolution can give you. It is as if you have to crawl up and along the branches to accept and experience the various worlds, which all the time your soul has grasped but the mind has not yet accepted; this is where the Tree of Knowledge handicaps your greater realization or intuition. All the time in this journey you have to see and accept the Tree of Life and not be sidetracked by the Tree of Knowledge. Once more, as with my warning of the voices, you will know when this is correct as the soul is in command and that is in the Head centre.

As I/we look on the movement of the Homo sapiens in the 21st century, we see so many Beings that are ready for this understanding, but maybe because of their intelligence or knowledge are, to a certain degree, loath to take the next step. There seems to be nobody to help, but eventually they will realize that this time the answer is not in books or the church/mosque but in themselves. They will hear the voice of the Lord, as mentioned in your holy book, as so many before you have done, but hopefully now will realize what it is and why it has happened – how your higher self/soul has penetrated the mind, and at last the mind has directed the brain and a conscious understanding has penetrated the Being. So we, in the Hierarchy, can feel that one more little spark of light is finding its way home and so, as we are emerging into the 21st century, it is relevant that we move our understanding from the physical into the mental.

Chapter 10

WHAT OF THE TREE OF LIFE

Many are asking the question 'What of the Mind?', 'What is it?', 'Where is it?', and maybe 'Why is it?'. Through evolution this is surely a necessary development and for a number of years now the words psychiatry and psychology have been brandished about. These Beings have, dare I say, cottoned on to something: many in a logical, academic way, but nevertheless they have had thoughts that have enabled them to progress ideas, make statements and some to develop treatments and medicines to progress their understanding of the mind. Hopefully at the end of this century they will be able to cure the general dis-ease of the physical body through mind techniques and understanding. This is evolution, this is progress. I would like to put a pointer here and direct your attention/mind to what a great teacher said 2,000 years ago – 'In my Father's house there are many mansions'. Why did He say this and what did it mean?

If we trace the progression of Homo sapiens we have to admit that we are not the same Being now as we were then. Possibly by the end of this Age we will be different again, so can't we say as time goes by that we have developed and changed our physical body? I do not have to enunciate the many changes that have taken place; but now we can look back and see the great progress that has enabled us to keep our physical body in good order, it is surely time that we investigate the Mind and realise it too has an important part to play, perhaps the most important part.

We have first of all to accept that we are dealing with another form of vibration – not physical or 3rd dimensional, not something we can see and feel, but something we can sense. This is the whole essence of the 4th dimension, so the mind, like the etheric body, to all intents and purposes is invisible. But we are well aware of it and soon realize that when it is not at ease the whole of our physical body can be affected. Now the mind controls the brain and the brain controls the body; the higher self or soul controls the mind – hence mind, body and soul.

As the great energy or light penetrates the planet, so it, in its turn, sends that light through to the Beings on its planet. It takes aeons of time before some of that light gets to the 'inhabitants' of the planet – mineral, vegetable and animal worlds – but each in its turn is imbued with this energy and, like seeds, begins to grow. So this great energy, that I'd like to call spirit, infiltrates the emerging Homo sapiens in varying degrees – tiny fractions of light/energy manage to open up one of those mansions. Can you see how the pattern and the Purpose emerges – as the spirit ignites the soul, so the soul directs the mind and the mind communicates with the relevant part of the brain that ultimately brings the idea into consciousness?

Now according to the degree of this direction you get the various interpretations of that instruction. As the energy becomes more forceful it is then able to move on to more power and a greater understanding is produced. This we might call the 4th dimension, movement from the 3rd to the 4th, and as mentioned before a different interpretation is forthcoming – colour takes its turn and that develops into sound. Music is, therefore, the highest understanding of the make-up of the planet, it is that sound that actually creates in the first place and why it is said 'In the beginning was the word (sound) and the word was with God' (or the Universal Power).

As each of you is developing into a 4th dimensional Being, you are/ will be aware of this vibration and a new attitude begins to move into your Being. You can begin to see why humanity is so varied and the reason why they are different. Most are firmly fixed in that 3rd dimensional mansion, fuelled by the power of the solar plexus with all its emotional overtones. But you have moved on, not superficially but evolutionarily, and hence are different from those Homo sapiens. How much we owe to this power of thought/energy that ignites the new mansions when they are ready, and a different Being, to a degree, is born, still using its knowledge of the 3rd dimension but with wisdom and making use of the 4th to give a greater realisation, hence explanation, of the world.

The world teachers of the future will give a deeper understanding of the parables in your holy book. Of course this book was written for spiritual understanding, but so much has been used as material explanation and the point has been lost. One hears the question 'How can God allow so much suffering and hate? He is therefore not a loving God'. But the Universal Spirit/Sound is perfect and, unfortunately, immediately it is created it is influenced by the surrounding vibration or colour ray; hence an imperfect thought is born. God cannot be blamed for the evil that is in the world. Man has created it by his selfishness and misunderstanding, either innocently or intentionally, and must take the responsibility for what is. If you trace nearly everything, whether physical or mental, back to the source you will find ego or self-aggrandisement at the bottom of it – the feeling that I am right and you are wrong – but as you move up or along the branches of the Tree of Life you begin to see it is the aspect or the vision of that particular question that comes to the mind, and you begin to see, as you say, 'Things in a different light'.

All this helps you as a Being to get a greater understanding of your part and development, and you realize that God in its 3rd dimensional colours has taken the brunt of your unhappiness, or viciousness – 'Forgive them Lord, they know not what they are doing/thinking' your Teacher said, and had they understood, that great thought or Being would not have been persecuted. He did not blame anyone because he knew it was inevitable that many did not understand – how could they on that 3rd dimension? But those who had moved on and took the call of this Teacher became disciples and World Teachers themselves, often meeting the same fate, I'm afraid, because of the same reason – their 4th mansion had received the light whereas the others were still occupying the 3rd mansion. All this, hopefully, gives you a greater understanding of the Purpose of Life, a quiet feeling of detachment that helps to make the journey more understandable. It comes under the umbrella of that word Why, and helps to give the explanation of one of the greatest parables given in your holy book – that of the Prodigal Son.

This explains the whole gamut of evolution, from the spark of light, spinning out into the universe, collecting all that is there, becoming matter, as you understand it, and ultimately with the nucleus of that spark/ spirit feeling the pull or direction back to its source. He made a lovely story of it, of man leaving home to go out into the world to experience all that is necessary – how else can you learn? You read some books but it does not sink in until you are ready and have absorbed that experience and then a different realization comes to mind. But sooner or later each of you begins to want/realize that what you started with is really what you need, and you feel the compulsion to return to your source.

So this story of evolution repeats itself time and again, but each time as it completes the circle it moves on a bit and another cycle is developed and again completed in the same way, all the time perfecting the understanding of the Godhead and acquiring a little more of the Plan and Purpose of the journey of evolution. So again perhaps you can see how and why you change as Beings through many lives, all the time experiencing and reacquainting yourself for the greater knowledge, understanding and acceptance of your fellow Homo sapiens, moving all the time towards the brotherhood of man, and ultimately to love – that is the pinnacle of the Godhead.

Love is the most difficult to achieve, accept and understand. It changes as you move your experience through the centres: love on the yellow ray/ Solar Plexus is different from the green ray/Heart because you should now have the answer. It is taking a different degree or vibration and hence displays itself in a different way – a greater dedication emerges and the selfish, emotional side of it begins to take a step backwards. As you move on through the centres it shows itself as love of humanity, a dedication to others, and that power is transmuted to the brotherhood of man and the ultimate perfection of the Homo sapiens as displayed by the Master Jesus.

Everything works on a pattern based on the development of spiritual awareness, and as this dawns on the Being so ultimately a different human Being emerges. It takes aeons of time, but as I have mentioned before, that in itself is one's own development. So many of you in the 21st century are moving into this Heart centre: you will feel the power of that centre and hence will glean a more tolerant and deeper understanding of your fellow Homo sapiens. Still decisions have to be made as far as you personally are concerned as to what you can accept and reject. Mistakes are inevitable but if you can admit your error and not refuse to see that you have taken a wrong decision, then once more you are moving on to a deeper understanding of yourself and your fellow men. This then develops the broader understanding of Humanity as a whole, and we touch on the Purpose and use of the United Nations.

At first in the uniform of the League of Nations the idea was absorbed from the Universal Source, but like a lot of ideas it was not strong enough to survive. However, that seed has been sown and lay dormant for a while, ultimately showing itself as the United Nations – a little stronger this time I'm pleased to say but still very weak and tender. Will mankind see its purpose this time, or will it get crushed and broken only to have another period of waiting for a stimulating force/Being to develop the idea once again? If man could only realize that the Tree of Life has many branches each part of the very essence of that tree, and each and everyone of you is part of or is one of those branches. Can't you see how the different branches are produced?

We come now to try and accept and understand the various Races that are present on the planet/tree: how each is a branch of that tree; each comes from the actual source but is a different branch, a different aspect of the Universal Whole. The idea of the United Nations is the root formation of that Tree of Life. It is trying to unite mankind, not as the same Homo sapiens but as different Beings, and gradually through time to bring the Brotherhood of Man into fruition, thus showing how each race is a part of the whole, a necessary part for that tree to maintain its dignity and beauty. Each is necessary and without which the tree would not be complete and the race accepted for what it is – part of that great source/idea that was the original spark of the Universal Power itself. Some branches are new and are just sprouting out, others are older and stronger and are part of a bough of the tree – each different and yet part of the formation of the Tree of Life. What a beautiful idea that God created in the Garden of Eden.

Chapter 11

SELF-REALISATION

Today, with your knowledge and development of how and why the glorious trees have formulated, giving you the very life-force/oxygen that you require to take evolution on to a greater expression of the Godhead, hold on to the idea and the story of the Tree of Life; see it for what it is, and what it will be; give your love on its higher vibration to water and to protect this very beautiful tree that once again is trying to grow and show itself in the minds and understanding of humanity itself. And so we move on to the exploration of this Being we call Homo sapiens.

Science, through intelligence and knowledge, is helping to develop the brain in order that the mind, directed by the soul, can bring forth a greater realisation of the Being and hence the Universe as a whole. As the 5th Root Race shows itself, a different kind of interpretation will come into manifestation, all the time opening yet another mansion. I hope you are beginning to see the pattern that is emerging, each idea or seed of the Universal Mind showing itself in humanity, opening up that throat centre and bringing in the blue vibration using the sound that corresponds to that centre and hence a deeper realisation of the Purpose of life.

I have just touched on sound, but like colour it takes its place and gently moves up the spectrum to develop and strengthen the vibration of whichever centre the Being has achieved – as colour is related to the rainbow so sound is developed through the musical scale, and here you can see why music is of prime importance to the progression of the planet and to the Homo sapiens likewise. May I relate the musical scale to the seven colours, starting with Tonic Solfar names: Doh = the Red centre, Ray the Orange, Me the Yellow centre (Solar Plexus – a strong mental colour predominant in many flowers – the pollen and stamens in most are yellow and they are the basis on which the flower exists), on to Green (Heart) but this makes a great step forward as this centre develops. At first there is Yellow overshadowing it and you have the yellow green in grass, but as the understanding develops a touch of Blue creeps in and you get the Blue green or Turquoise – rather like its musical counterpart Fah. It is not quite sure which way to go, a difficult time in the light of evolution of that Being, but when it gets the understanding then that is the opening up of the realisation of the 4th dimension. Then on to the Blue (throat) Soh ray that will enable you to look on life in a broader and deeper way beginning to ask questions and getting the answers yourself, hence moving you into the power and understanding of the Third eye – Indigo, Lah that gives the power to that Eye enabling you to become more of a visionary – a kind of seeing that is deeper and broader than the average Homo sapiens. Finally, Te the centre at the top of the head.

I like to see and think of you Beings, as you become 4th dimensional, as musical instruments; as you pluck at the strings of your violin or harp, each begins to play its own musical sound and the vibration moves through time and space to the great garden of self–realisation – the sound source of all creation, universal or planetary. If music be the source of life, play on. From it the sound that is individual to each Being is the main source of the whole vibration of the individual Homo sapiens, and maybe you can see how important, used in the right way, mantras are - Om Mani Padne Aum sends out a call or colour ray that enables us to hear the cry and hopefully pick it up and reply to it. Out of this comes scientific discoveries: the understanding of D.N.A., writing of the philosophies, painting and music, that opens the way to the inspirational interpretation of the Universe as a whole. So you see how each Being is, broadly speaking, moving into perfect sound/colour, the light that is the wholeness of creation and the sound that is the silence in which we live and move and have our Being.

As you move along this path you begin to see it is necessary to know and accept where the main centres of the Etheric are and ultimately to be able to play them as an instrument, giving you access to healing and spiritual philosophy. You meet up with others on this path as they will be attracted to you, and you listen and learn from their experiences, building a relationship that helps to move you on your way, all the time experiencing the journey that, through many lives, will bring you back home – Prodigal Son.

Maybe I should touch here on the Will of God, which is the inner conviction of you as a Being now being directed by the soul – that precious part of you that has managed to get into incarnation and can direct the Homo sapiens, in the material sense, to help further the expansion and evolution of the planet as a whole. Here it is very necessary to realise that your 3rd dimensional life is still of great importance to yourself and mankind. You are helping the development of the planet in a material sense, and allowing that thought or spark of the Will of God to penetrate the mind and so give the go ahead to the brain to put into practice the new idea; so, as is often referred to, the left and right brain are playing their part in your development and, as I've mentioned before, the group or planet as a whole.

In the Aquarian Age there will be many Beings who have accepted the need to understand and to know how to use these facilities. This is the goal of the Age of the Mind – the Aquarian Age. You know a great deal as to how your physical body works, but what of the mind? Where does IT come in, and what is meant by 'Mind over Matter'? So often it is said 'I was of two minds', or 'I had a feeling that', etc., all very profound statements which tell you that the Mind is the greatest development, and it has taken aeons of time to, perhaps we may say, bring it to the surface.

As the Beings move on to this vibration the need for language will be less and direct communication on a mind to mind conception will take place. Language can be misinterpreted and often causes great trouble and misunderstanding, but if a telepathic link can be employed there is less likely to be mistakes made. As I have mentioned so often, all this must be achieved oneself – a deep conviction and realisation that this is the path to Universal Brotherhood, all done under the umbrella of love on its 4th dimensional understanding. As you progress through evolution you lighten yourself, bringing your physical body to a lighter vibration through vegetarianism, and as I've mentioned before, this isn't just avoiding meat but the realisation as to why the meat of an animal, especially those killed in terror in your slaughterhouses, will keep the density of the body low. As your sensitivity develops so your vehicle must be tuned to cope with this, and the meat of animals is of a different vibration to what you now require having sorted out your physical - not because vegetarianism is in vogue but because you have a strong feeling that this is right for you. Here the mind is giving a clear direction and has become strong enough to influence you consciously.

Many true vegetarians were ridiculed years ago, but they kept to their belief and now you can see there are many who follow this path, and it is accepted by those who would have shunned the whole idea in the past. You can stand back and see how evolution works on various levels - back to the escalator, a good analogy to try to explain the development of mankind.

All of this is really a general releasing of the coatings we collect through many lives and don't dispense of them but have to deal with the complexities in each incarnation - rather like Salome and the 7 veils we gradually throw away until we become pure enough to enter the Kingdom of God and our spirit is able to engulf itself in that beautiful heavenly perfection. We all have a long way to go, but nevertheless we are on our way. Nothing can stop us, evolution is the clarion call but it takes so long before we are sensitive enough to hear it, and next we come to the touchy one - Religion.

I wonder why, when it is and has been so important to you in your many lives - like vegetarianism you have needed it - all the great teachers have been or are religious? It teaches you discipline and acceptance of a power greater than your own understanding, and it brings you to the acknowledgement of the necessity of that teaching, no matter what path you take. Why argue about one form of teaching with another? Can't you see the ultimate idea is the same? All acknowledge the Universal Power, regardless of what you call it - God, Allah, Jehovah - but as you progress along your path to realisation and eventually to self-realisation, you begin to see this and a great acceptance takes over. You see how you who argued before can now discuss and listen to others, seeing that deep down the great Teacher is saying 'Love one another'. Understand and appreciate others that are interpreting the philosophy of life in maybe a slightly different way, and when you get to that form of realisation then you are ready to take off the next veil and the question becomes what have I learned and truly accepted from this religion?

As I have mentioned before, we are now seeing that we are ready to give in our own right and not use religion as a means to pray for help and expect to get an answer to our wants. We must stand up and deal with our lives ourselves, but we must remember that religion has taught us to eventually do this. When you make this big decision it must be done with love and thanks and not, as I hear so many who, of course, are not yet ready to move out of religion, have unpleasant things to say about its narrow-mindedness, etc. They are painting a picture of themselves and showing how clearly they are not yet ready to move into the philosophy of Spiritual Realisation – in some ways more difficult as you are on your own. So you see, just as for the planet there is a Purpose and a Plan so you too have yours.

Now through this incarnation you should stop occasionally and look back at your life and try to see the Purpose of it, and more especially to start to think of how you are going to direct your next incarnation. This will be a great help to you on your return as you will have a knowing as to what you want to do. I'm sure you have heard and read of many Beings who will tell that from an early age they knew what they wanted to do, often turning down chances to do something else and often they will achieve a better attitude and peace of mind by holding on to their dream. So we experience Religion in its depth only eventually to move out of it into our own understanding, but always acknowledging the necessity of it. Like so many experiences, we will find that although we have had many religious lives we feel the need to move on and we begin to explore the 'Arts'. These again take their order and often we move into writing stories here unbeknown or accepted by you. You will get a form of inspiration, you have a knowing about your story which you can't quite understand, ideas and situations emerge and you now have a form of direction or inner voice that has taken over.

All the Arts are subject to this and most Beings think it is their ideas, but actually you have moved on to another vibration that holds a new interpretation in words, painting and music - really all the different sounds that formulate into different groups producing literature, painting and music. Most of these Beings have relinquished 'religion', not in an anti way, as I've mentioned, but are moving on to a different field of understanding and interpretation of the beauty of the Planet and all that it stands for.

I think I have said before that the writer thinks IT, the painter sees IT, the musician hears IT, but the mystic knows IT. Can you see the same stages of development? All the time the soul is able to influence the mind and so bring into being a different experience that will enable the brain to produce the concrete manifestation of the Sounds of the Spheres. When you move from meditation to inspiration this is inevitable, your head centre is now open as a flower/lotus and ready to collect what you call information from other sources. But having achieved this, can you bring it down to manifestation? With practice and acceptance this is possible, but it takes many lives before a direct communication can develop – again many artists do this as they have earned this great privilege, but do they know why? Karma? Here again we come to the question that the inspiration received eventually has an explanation, and once that stage is achieved, recognised and accepted, then the Being is ready to move on.

Chapter 12

THOUGHT TRANSFERENCE

All the time I am trying to point out that the mind has to bring all this to consciousness. On the way distractions and interference occur and in some cases a muddled product is the result, but as Handel heard the Music of the Spheres he was able, because of his knowledge of music, to write it down and so brought the sound into consciousness.

So, as we progress through Religion and then the Arts, what next? The general collection of all this manifests itself into a teaching that will use the dedication of Religion, now with true understanding that enables it to be painted into a philosophy that some Homo sapiens are searching for. As you journey through this life many difficulties and unhappinesses occur, and this is when you need something to fall back on. Some Homo sapiens turn to religion and that is satisfactory for them – they feel it gives them the necessary explanation and the answers to what they need, but others have a deep conviction that there is a Plan and a Purpose to their lives, and when difficulties occur this gives them the strength needed – a feeling you are not alone, that there is something always ready to give you hope and enables you to go on.

Those Beings that have no Religion or Philosophy are very often the ones that become ill – mentally or physically. They feel that life is not worth living or struggling for and so give up, but the others that pray to God or feel the fulfilment of an understanding seem to survive. Once more, according to the stage of evolution you have achieved, you will get the strength of this calling, all the time sensing the need for an interpretation of this wonderful life and planet that you have come to call home. So now you are beginning to experience that inner 'Peace which passeth all understanding'.

You'll feel more and more the need for detachment and a need to be on your own; if you are married this can be very difficult for your partner and can often lead to complications. If you are fortunate to be with someone who has a similar attitude to life then you are very lucky, but actually you would have earned this and it would be your karma – you see this form of philosophy gives an explanation to so many of life's experiences. One of the things that helps as you move on your way is to be able to get some sort of answer to the question Why? So many Beings get mixed up and spend years trying to understand why certain things have happened to them that it makes them mentally ill; even if you try to explain this form of understanding they would not or could not accept it. They are not as far up the escalator as yourself; hopefully you can see the reason for their predicament and now have to give yourself that time and understanding that is necessary to develop your whole Being.

Perhaps now you can see the need for groups and societies, the joy of meeting and being with people of like mind. Here, ideas and feelings are exchanged, some hopefully a little ahead of your own, but this is where you learn and accept so much. For the first time you feel you are with people who speak the same language as yourself. There is no disagreement but an exchange of ideas in some things that you have been given through your soul/mind connection but have kept to yourself. Perhaps in the past you have experienced some of them and have been made to feel ridiculous which has sent you into yourself, so now you are very careful to whom you disclose your feelings and interpretations of life as you see it. You stay for the necessary time it takes you to work your way through this society/school and then once more when you are ready, and that may not be in this incarnation, you set off on another journey that will bring you eventually 'home'.

Quite a story isn't it? But a fulfilling one, and this all comes naturally – no studying in the material sense, in fact the more you read often a bigger muddle you will get into. The 4th dimension has different 'books' and when you get there you will find that it is thought transference that is 'the book' and that takes quite a while to read. Let us take 'a page' in this 4th dimensional book and we find the language is vibration expressing itself by thought – not words expressing themselves into sentences – quite different don't you see? Towards the end of the 21st century, hopefully, there will be many such Beings who will find this language/thought transference quite natural. They can, of course, speak but use the voice much less and the sound of the speech will be transferred to the mind – hence thought transference. Once more I would add this is the course of evolution. A form of group/society has already developed, and these Beings in incarnation at the present time, of course, are finding it very difficult to be accepted and understood. They are considered anti-social, often referred to the psychologist who naturally will not understand them.

However, everything has to start somewhere – vegetarians, as I've mentioned before, were made to feel outcasts and misunderstood, but as you are aware, now there are numbers of them and they are accepted as part of the community; so try to see and understand this different development and accept it as the natural progression of evolution. If you, as a Being, cannot do this it is not to say it is wrong or impossible; words complicate and some Beings are unable to express simply what they mean. They get misunderstood and much develops from it, but not so when the mind, that it is closer to the soul, takes over and direct transference is the result.

I think you will note that during this incarnation you have a desire to do something but often that thought is tampered with and a different instruction is the result. When you are able to discern the thought power and realise that all the arts are driven by it, then once more you have achieved a further revelation in the field of evolution. I am writing this book by means of thought transference, as I did with others, but of course it is very difficult to find the student who is able and ready to share in this task. Again, the quality of the material is limited by the quality of the instrument used – isn't this so in your material life? Two mathematicians can have a different concept from that of two others.

So thought transference is the key to the 21st century. It is the means whereby those Beings who have, through evolution, recognised that there is a further understanding as to how man progresses on this long road to perfection. Science has made great steps forward in the understanding of the physical body, but now is the turn of the mental or mind. Where does this spark of inspiration come from? And how is it to be used? As I have mentioned before, to put it simply means one more mansion is opened to humanity, and the door is there for those to open who have the understanding and acceptance to open it. Another realisation and revelation is there for you to experience, and as the light of that understanding emerges so too does a greater realisation of what Homo sapiens can further achieve. This is not physical but mental – funnily enough what mankind has been using since the beginning of time but not accepted as a spiritual direction, not realised as the essence of the holy power of the spirit – 'Holy, Holy, Holy, Lord God Almighty, heaven and earth are full of your Glory' – a quote from one of your great hymns.

How were these sayings written? Where did they come from? And what did they mean? The answer is in thought transference, where all the great works of philosophy have come from. The Being has knowingly or unknowingly heard and acknowledged the thoughts of these Beings, or maybe vibrations, that have moved on up the escalator of evolution. Some have seen, some have sensed, but that power of thought has been strong enough to make or enable them to translate it into words, and those Beings have been able to bring forth the word of God. So now in this 21st century, it will not be the few but the many who will be able to hear and understand.

The important thing is to understand and not just accept. As I am directing this my student is writing it down with a clear mind not in trance form but just as an ordinary natural communication. This will continue to develop in more and more of humanity, as it rightly should; as you learn and feel your centres opening up so naturally you too will open up and become the beautiful lotus on top of the pond of spiritual understanding. This now is the development of the mind over matter, the mental over the physical, and the progression of the higher self or soul communication with the mind/brain.

As you feel and sense this happening in your head centre it is the true connection with the spirit – that little bit of the Godhead that you have brought into incarnation, and indeed what has enabled you to exist as a Being in this form. When IT decides to leave you are what you call dead. This spiritual communication will take you on to further dimensions and understandings, gradually releasing you from the ties of the third dimensional world. Taking in the field of nature in all its beauty, you will need and feel the silence; then you can hear the sounds of the air, and in that atmosphere of quietness you will hear the words of those who have moved on and learn the greatness of further intelligences. This is not messages from loved ones; you will not be given instructions as to how to run your earthly life; but you will be given answers to questions on life itself.

So Thought Transference is my teaching for the 21st century, as perhaps I might say Meditation was the message for the twentieth. It means that as/if you have developed the stillness of the mind through meditation, you should be ready to touch the vibration of sound which is thought transference. All the great teachings that have come down through the ages have been delivered in this way; each era has sent forth a further development or realisation of the Creator God, and once this has been delivered then those Beings that are able, through their understanding, interpret it for Humanity itself. This is where so much gets mixed up, as I am sure you can understand, but we are grateful to the few who have managed, through evolution, to reach the stage whereby thought transference can be used.

Now in the 21st century more Beings have reached this stage and, hopefully, through their ability to transmit this information, it will obviously be spread around into a wider area. The Spiritual Hierarchy have sent out this direction to the Teachers of Humanity, and it is our job to find and develop those Beings that have the potential to learn and accept this further understanding. We amass small groups of three and build their colour rays so that eventually they will be able to take on this work, ultimately working alone, but on the spiritual level always in communication with the 4th dimensional Beings/Teachers.

What have we to communicate? First and foremost, the great understanding of knowing yourself; to be able to sense and see your strengths and weaknesses; to understand those that are not as far along the path as yourself; to put a hand out where you think it is necessary, but not to enforce or direct another's life. Each and every one has to move along the Road of Realisation, often taking wrong turnings and finding their way back again. Too much is being done to help humanity in one way, as kindness can be a means of stopping progress. So, emotionalism has to stop and understanding must take its place – here we move onto the next stage of the 5th dimension when the Being will develop spiritual sight, and in that way will be able to hear and see.

As your physical senses have developed through the ages so will your spiritual, and hence there will be many who can work as your Christ – or Teacher Jesus – did all those years ago, sent as a World Teacher like others that have come after him i.e. Mohammed, each giving out, through Thought Transference, the teaching of the Masters of the 4th dimension. As I've said before, governed by their own instruments – nationally and environmentally all Sons of God – but some have got a little nearer to home and hence hear the Creator and see Him in all His Glory, and in their own perfection will ultimately be engulfed into the great Love of the Godhead.

I am trying to give you a reason for life itself, to show how there is a Plan and a Purpose, that evolution is the key, accepting and rejecting the difficulties of the journey back Home to the Source of Life itself. It is inevitable that what is taken from the Godhead must be returned, the circle of evolution is the same on the spiritual level as on the material. It is all relative, and once this form of teaching is accepted you can understand your fellow Homo sapiens, once more may I say, where you/they have got to on the escalator of life.

This all comes under the University of Life. What qualifications do you require to be accepted? Again, as I have mentioned before, very different ones to that of the 3rd dimension. There is only one 'subject' – Spiritual Attainment. As the Beings concerned move forward under the umbrella of the teachings of this University, they will take many incarnations before they eventually achieve their diploma, but qualify they will in the end. And this time more beings will be giving out the Teaching of Light in the Understanding and Universal Realisation necessary to help that section of Humanity that is ready to hear and understand, according to their evolution, what is needed of them to help speed on the spiritual development of this planet.

As more and more Beings open the window of this teaching, so a greater acceptance will emerge of the true meaning of 'Love Thy Neighbour' by Beings that, through their earthly lives, have felt and seen for themselves the necessity of giving to their fellow Beings and not expecting something in return. One sees too much taking and not a thought of giving in the world today, but as mankind moves on then it becomes automatic that you help your fellow Beings, not only with service but with money as well. It is often quite difficult for a Being to give his savings to help humanity. That is something quite deep in the feelings, but you will learn and find out that the more you give on any level the more you will receive. Of course you have to have that true dedication and true conviction before this is granted.

Chapter 13

FINDING A WAY

Once more all of this comes naturally. There is no pressure, it takes time and evolution before the 'penny drops'. So now I would say that each being must understand how their Etheric Body works. This is the most important part of your Being. It draws in power to the physical and releases power. It is the breathing centre, if you like, of the physical body, on the whole controlled by seven centres, each responsible for different sections of the body, and so important that immediately one or the other is not working properly then illhealth is the result in the physical body. Your medical people will eventually acknowledge this via the psychiatrists and psychologists; some of them are beginning to think about this and, of course, with the aid of students from the University of Life, a greater conclusion will develop. If you take a pendulum and slowly, slowly pass it towards the physical you will see it move as it crosses the etheric body – this means there is a power there and proves to you that something has been touched.

Now it is important to learn to strengthen this etheric body by mentally sensing and accepting its presence. At first one may use the imagination to build this oval/egg – shaped body , but gradually with practice it will feel a part of you, just as in your arms and legs. You can soon sense a hurt in your physical body, so your sensitivity will develop and you will be aware of part of the etheric body that is hurt/holed, and then through thought you put your mind to repairing and making it strong again – like the spider repairs its web – hence no wrong vibrations can penetrate the physical body and cause dis-ease to that Homo sapiens. If you talk to a person who has had his leg amputated he will tell you that he feels it is still there, so much so that he often will put his hand there to feel the leg. The etheric leg cannot be amputated, it is made up of different material to the physical and stays on a short while when the physical body is dead. One more part of your body that needs to be learned about and understood.

The East has had so much to offer on this level – their whole attitude to death, for example, is based mostly on re-incarnation. They accept the fact that the soul must be respected and helped on its way to the world beyond – the ancient Egyptians knew this and much can be learned and read about their custom. So much today is ignored of the past, but a wise person takes what is good and leaves what is bad. What the West is about is through science to give an explanation and a realisation that there are other dimensions to explore and understand – another world is there which needs different equipment to try to get to it. But just an acceptance must be there of the soul and the etheric body, and once this is achieved then the new dimension has been penetrated. So let us for the moment think of the soul that in 'death' has been released from its physical 'home'. Very often during the whole of its earthly life it has been ignored – like a little voice in a box trying to let you know it is there, but rejected and refused acknowledgement. Eventually it manages to be heard/felt and for a second it can penetrate the Higher Mind, but then that takes no notice and the message is misinterpreted by the lower mind. How many lives does it take before it is strong enough to be listened to, let alone acted upon?

The West is trying to understand and get an explanation for this, whilst the East just accepts and uses some ritual to give it shape. This is why it is so important that when 'death' takes place there is quiet, but this is far from so as many get upset, bundle the body away to a mortuary and have little communication with it, often not wishing to see it as they are so afraid of death and dying. The East can show you a thing or two here but, of course, like so many things it often is dealt with in a hysterical way – just as that soul has great difficulty in getting into the physical world in birth so, likewise, it has difficulty getting out. Like the caterpillar that changes into a butterfly, as the soul 'flies' away it is in a different form, but still is/was that Being in the first place.

The Buddha makes reference to this in his teachings. The East accepts this but the West dismisses it as mere fantasy – whatever that means! If more of this understanding could be accepted, it would help Beings so much when their loved ones pass on. All the emotional hurt could be helped and this would often give time and place to what has really happened – not wishing the Being back but giving it a chance to fly away to experience another flower/dimension and feel free of the heavy load of that physical body.

As thought transference becomes more accepted, understood and experienced, so all the heavy mental stresses fly away and that will take away the fears and tensions that today are experienced by so many: the whole Being begins to strengthen, the Etheric body does not have such a battle with unhappy/wrong thoughts, it does not get penetrated as easily and hence disease is averted. As I have mentioned before, the 21st century is all about the Mind, and as time goes on more will get a greater realisation of how that wonderful machine/computer, the brain, really works. This then will take Homo sapiens on to a new 'religion' called Contemplation. It has its own way of 'teaching': it must justify itself, but gradually as the Being moves forward different pictures begin to evolve, a greater acceptance of all that is/was, contentment emerges and self-realisation is the outcome. I'm sure you've met those Beings who seem to have a gentleness but strength in their personality. Some will know what it is but others will try to give you the reason why they feel this way - so contemplation and contentment are the product of meditation, and self-realisation the goal of the inner realisation that ultimately leads to the true understanding of the purpose of life.

Often you hear Beings asking 'Why am I here? What am I doing?' But here they stop and don't allow themselves to go just a little bit further, too nervous to open the door of that new mansion that is there to accept and explore. One thing that must be avoided is allowing contentment to move into complacency, as then the Being just floats along and the exploration of the 4th dimension just does not develop further. But, like everything in this teaching, there is no hurry and if that is all that can be achieved in this incarnation so be it. Often that contentment will lead the Being to develop further the practical necessities of life – helping humanity and dedicating itself to the contentment of giving, expressing their thoughts in writing, painting, music, moving into the field of science and medicine – so necessary to advance now that the 21st century has dawned. It has stayed too long in a groove only seeing the narrow margins and not allowing itself to broaden the field that lies ahead; it surely must listen and discuss with those who see the Being as a whole and not just one piece or part of the physical.

Diagnosis is the field of the doctor, but until he can relate to Thought Transference and get the true help from a different channel he is stuck with this analytical diagnosis. One thing, of course, that always stops this is lack of proof, and on one level this must be noted, but in many cases the ancients i.e. Chinese, have already given that proof but the modern doctor will not accept it – maybe it is not written in a language that he can understand. Homeopathy has much to offer, Asclepius, a Greek philosopher and great healer, left so much; if only they would read, learn and take what is needed for the present century. All the branches of ideas have to be assimilated, tried and the best of them used to help mankind develop a greater understanding of who they are and what they are made up of. And finally, when this has been achieved, the great acknowledgement of the true Being is forthcoming – the Etheric – not the physical at all. That beautiful veil that drapes the body and turns it into the glorious colour rays of the Universal power – there all the time but not recognised or accepted. Inspired writers such as Blavatsky and Alice Bailey knew where their information came from. If only the learned gentlemen would read their work it would save them so much time as ultimately they will come to the same conclusion; they can put it in their language, and mankind can move on to a greater realisation of the Purpose of this form of life itself. Remember I am writing this for those of you who have reached a certain stage of evolution on the turquoise ray, can sound the AUM in the head centre, know how to use/feel the centres of your Being as a musician plays his violin/flute (like the great god Pan, but he only played 4 notes on his pipe as the 3 below had been eliminated by evolution, i.e. the lower centres).

Now I have to mention here that thought transference is only able to take place when the Being has reached quite an advanced stage in its evolution, but it must be noted in order to direct the thought into this form of expression - hopefully towards the end of the 21st century there will be many able to use this form of telepathy. I am giving this information in order to help those who are already able to use this form of connection with the 4th dimension - Beings who, through evolution, have a true understanding of what this is all about. Hopefully, some of you are beginning to see the Plan, and later the Purpose will come into your understanding.

As the Being makes its way back towards the central force then it will begin to use the energy of the ultimate power itself. Now you will no doubt hear and read about mind control in its mental capacity and will give this your concentration and acceptance. I'm sure you can see that to control the mind of Homo sapiens on the 3rd dimension is a great responsibility and can be dangerous. Your parapsychologists have been doing this for a while under the medical curtain and results, in many cases, have been successful; but these doctors have to answer to their peers and, hopefully, accept the responsibility of what they are doing. It would, of course, be so much better if they knew the reason why they can affect the patient in this way; I'm sure some do, but these are Beings who realise they are actually dealing with the Etheric Body of the patient and understand how very important this is to the Being. Once this mental control gets into the hands of less evolved ignorant Beings it becomes dangerous - just as Mediums in the Spiritualist Movement can/will not always connect with spirits who are on the right path. But, as I have mentioned, I'm speaking to those Beings who are moving up the escalator, have a greater vista of all that is/was, and now are not connecting with man-to-man so to speak, but are able to link with 4th dimensional teachers. They will develop the higher mind to connect with the lower, and hence the Being will become inspired and able to deliver information that is necessary to help mankind on its next stage of realisation. The Prophets - the Spiritual Philosophers - did it, and now more of the human family are ready to touch on this different approach to life, in a detached way but with a great love for Humanity, each accepting that this is all built via the Etheric Body which, of course, by now they completely accept. Some will sense this telepathic link, some will hear it and some will know it; this then will give this small section of Humanity a greater voice.

None of this work can be made to happen. Meditation helps to still your mind in order that these Beings can make themselves heard, but when your vibration has reached that point of evolution then the Teacher will appear. The Buddha used the expression 'When the pupil is ready the Teacher will appear'. This statement is so well put. Like any material teacher 'They' are so happy and pleased when the light begins to shine forth, always looking and hoping for this to happen, but until that light of a certain stage of enlightenment shines forth they can only wait. No help is given until the self-realisation of the Being is established, then the journey of the higher mind becomes so strong it no longer questions the spiritual capacity, but the direction is there and the instruction moves firmly into the brain and hence into consciousness.

So it is my hope that this little book will be able to open the 'pages' of those who, through evolution, have reached the beginning of their journey back to the Universal power from which they have come, asking the questions 'Who am I? What am I? Where am I going?' Realising that chasing around the world, owning property, cars, etc. does not satisfy their inner self which is searching for peace, and knowing that somewhere inner realisation is there. It is so strong because your higher self is at last, after many lives, getting a grip of your Being and is making itself heard via the mind and brain. The Homo sapiens can only evolve in this way; more and more are now ready and able to take the next step forward. If you look at the history of the evolution of mankind you will accept, I think, that it has really been through ideas and 'inspiration' that the Beings have got to the present stage of development and understanding. As those ideas have become part of the Homo sapiens it has developed the physical body to bring that idea into material development. So what of your present situation?

The body now has become more agile, able to achieve so much more than thousands of years ago, and here you are with a brain/computer that is able to react to more refined instructions. So the operator/mind has now got stronger instruction from the source, and that in itself has been able to connect with the Universal power which you choose to call God. Up until now man has believed that he must worship the Beings that he used to call Gods; now he has settled for one God, but is also realising that he is himself becoming one - a gentle, loving creature, whose inner knowledge and love for all his fellow Beings is manifest in himself, becoming a World Teacher and able to accept and give forth the teachings of the Master Jesus with great humility and true understanding which he taught to 'Those that have ears to hear'.

Hopefully this kind of philosophy gives a greater understanding and realisation of what life on this planet is really about - dare I say, the creation of a Garden of Eden that was there at the beginning and is still there if mankind can find its way back to it. All that you need is here, but through greed and selfishness you have got lost, been mesmerised by the 'beautiful lights' and gone off track. But now more and more of you are realising that this is not the way, and through meditation, contemplation and an inner knowing you are making your way back to that garden of love, peace and beauty, but this time knowing why you must return and how to accept other dimensions, vibrations and energies that have to be understood and brought into your Being via that higher self. Hence Thought Transference, a communication that is as strong and real to you as speaking on a telephone (a little similar I may add), but now you do not just accept the telephone as an instrument, you know how it works.

Once this direct communication can be established by you then your whole etheric body will change, and hence you will change and become a more beautiful Being in Body, Mind and Soul - God the Father (the physical), God the Son (the mind) and God the Holy Spirit (the soul/ spirit). Once more the instructions have been there, but most have missed the direction. So you see I am trying to give you an explanation of why you are in incarnation and how it is possible to achieve a greater realisation of the Plan of this evolutionary system (I may add just one of many); but each of you as specks of light is contributing to the whole, and will also be part of that great light that will enable greater Beings to walk and live on this planet once again.

Chapter 14

AT LAST ACCEPTANCE

If you look back at the history of the planet you will read of various civilizations who worshipped Beings in some form – as I have mentioned they called them Gods – who came to them from 'on high', and they built Temples to them. These Beings were able to influence a few who were ready to take their vibration/ray, and themselves had a chance to open that new mansion I have alluded to before. Some used it wisely, others not so, but then again that would depend upon the stage of evolution they had achieved. So now you have your Churches/Mosques that play a similar part and once more there are those Beings who take and understand more than others, and these Beings will eventually 'leave' that protection and move out into the field of life that they must experience on their own for themselves (Prodigal Son). It is then, on this new experience or new energy, that you develop the questions that I have mentioned. However, this time you must find the answers for yourself and not get them from your Master – he is standing by to see how, after many incarnations, you are going to answer those questions and deal with the experiences that have come your way.

As you move on you then realise the God within – that great power that has overshadowed you all the time but you have not realised or accepted it. Now you begin to see why it was necessary for your soul to influence the mind in order to bring to consciousness (brain) the true realisation of the universal energy (God). Even as you are reading this tiny booklet it will help to revise and release some of your deepest thoughts. Now you can accept that others have trodden the Way ahead of you, making a pathway for you to meander along with thoughts and ideas that you have kept to yourself - as so often when voiced they have received a negative response and you have learned to dismiss or keep silent about them. This is where groups or societies are of great help because you meet Beings who are treading a similar path to yourself and, of course, must ask the same questions. Now you can voice your ideas and find them accepted, and in some cases an explanation is forthcoming.

This is the whole point of writing this account of your spiritual journey to a better realisation of this 4th dimensional world that you have now found: accepting and learning about the Etheric Body, using and working with the 7 centres of your Being - just as you have learned about the 7 colours (rainbow) and the 7 notes (octave), so you have the 7 power centres that open up to let in the energy of the Planetary Master. All of this takes time and evolution, it cannot be hurried, but you begin to associate the main power force in your Being to one of the centres more than the others. Most Beings are using their Solar Plexus - hence the emotionalism and selfishness that goes with it. The Buddha said 'Put out the fires of hatred, greed and delusion'. He was saying that the three lowest power centres have to be controlled, and to a degree have no further use, before you can move to the Heart centre that will begin to fulfil the giving and kindness so necessary for humanity and the Being itself. I have mentioned this before but would like to reinforce and point out how the energy force is so personal and necessary to the development of the Homo sapiens; each one will associate with and to a degree hold on to that centre that through evolution it has managed to achieve. When you have accomplished the necessary understanding of that centre, then you will move on to the next - this may take many lives or can be achieved quite quickly. But if Beings try to push themselves, make themselves participate in various breathing exercises and sound projections, which forces the power of the centres on to the next vibration before the Being has truly understood and dealt with the centre that they are rightfully on, this affects the whole body - physically, mentally and spiritually.

Always remember time is man-made and is not used, as such, in the spiritual world, hence in the 'eyes' of the Chela it is no-thing and merely moves on 'When the pupil is ready'. It is not a competition to see who gets to the end first, but a realisation that you are actually moving along this 4th dimensional 'road'. Give yourself the time to truly understand where you are on this journey, enjoy the company of those who are travelling with you, and begin to radiate that love that you have experienced so that you understand the purpose of the whole evolutionary journey.

At first the heart centre touches the understanding of love taught by the Hierarchy - the love of your fellow-men and the realisation that now you 'give' to mankind and do not take (solar plexus). It is a difficult step, one which humanity is really just beginning to accept. Much more is being done to help those on the lower point of that escalator as events in the world are showing; it is difficult for you as Beings to accept that, in spite of all your love and contribution, so much is going wrong. But if you can sit back and see what has been achieved, then some credit must be given to the problem as a whole. Can you see that those Beings who have moved to the Throat Centre (blue) are already showing their voice on the injustices of the planet - not being put off by those who wish to silence their cry? With the aid of your modern technology (T.V. etc.) much can be portrayed to the people as a whole, the cry is passed on to those who are ready and able to take this great torch of responsibility. Unfortunately this power or energy can ignite the two sides of the problem, so balance and the need for true realisation is required here or there will be more unrest which can lead to a backward step being taken.

Try, as you confront these difficulties, to focus your mind on the cause and not the effect. Hold your counsel and don't get brainwashed by those who love sensationalism. Here we return once more to what has been mentioned before - the ability to get that soul/mind communication and to have that sense of really knowing your own purpose in this life. As this moves on you will, in the fullness of time, start to touch the Ajna centre (indigo) and now this is a great experience as you will spiritually see, hear or sense the purpose of your life - not materially which will be of no interest. Here you begin to withdraw and succour the glory and beauty of life as a whole. It needs quiet contemplation, getting in touch with the 4th dimension and accepting that you, as a Being, are watched over and shown the new world of the 4th dimension. You may say here 'Who will be helping those that are struggling with their existence?' But I would say that is the job for the Teachers of the New Age. You will sense a feeling of power of understanding that is personal to you, more and more confidence shows its head and a picture/pattern emerges; in one way you will feel alone as your conception of life becomes broader and will not fit in with Humanity as a whole, but as more and more Homo sapiens move into this centre then the hope for the planet and mankind may be secured. You will feel this sensation in your 3rd eye; you may see the beautiful indigo drifting in and out, getting stronger each day as you yourself are realising what is happening. I return here again to my reason for writing this very simple booklet; to help let you know why these experiences occur, the reason for them, and the whole purpose of the need for each Being to know where they are in this great journey back to the 'Promised Land'.

Finally, as I am giving an explanation of the use of the Etheric Centres, let us just touch on the Head Centre – the Jewel in the Lotus, hidden for so many lives but maybe in this very incarnation just starting to open up; a gradual feeling of a link with some greater realisation/understanding that helps to give you an explanation of the Plan and Purpose of true existence. There surely must be a way to greater understanding? Others have found it, so why not you? All of this development comes from lives of experience, a lifting of the self to self-realisation, and a need to try and give yourself some sort of understanding of the Plan and Purpose, plus the power needed to direct and propel you on your way. So as we move up this mountain of self-realisation we see different vistas. As you can accept the view from an aeroplane is different from the view from your garden, it is larger, more expansive, just taking a different aspect of a similar area, our Being is made up of so many areas of existence – physical, mental and spiritual – each holding its own place but each part of the whole. As we journey on we begin to try to appreciate the Being as a whole and get on to the questions I have mentioned as to Why, Where and How – Why have we become such an interesting specimen of original thought? Where has this interesting thought evolved from? And how are we interpreting it?

Man is now trying to bring all of this together and reach, in his own way, an answer that is satisfactory for him. We begin to realise that all this is governed by the Mind and this, in itself, is connected with the soul. No wonder the Ancient Egyptians put so much emphasis on this soul! It was to them so important that they had rituals to this great source of power. Today we express the same idea in a different way – not by ritual and dogma, but by an acceptance of the life power that is a form of creation necessary for us when we reach a certain point in spiritual understanding. If and when you are ready to accept this you can see that all creation, whether animal, vegetable or mineral, is a part of the whole. Each has its part to contribute and play, everything is interdependent and has gradually evolved into the Being that is part of the whole, each dependent on each other, each necessary to each other, one sustaining the other.

Through time new species occur as they attract more light, and hence we are looking for the New Age Homo sapiens that is now beginning to show itself, becomes a more Christ-like Being, moving into that 'Peace that passeth all understanding' as taught by your Teacher for twenty centuries. He set that vibration into operation so that those who had ears to hear His words, those who could see the depth of His teaching, would have the material to carry on in the light of His knowledge. More and more Beings are ready to understand this teaching but need, through evolution, to be given more logical explanations, must find their own interpretation and not just accept the 'Word of the Lord'. Each Being will ultimately develop into a Christ-like soul – this is inevitable if you accept evolution. The 21st Century will move the Homo sapiens on as the Mind is developed and understood; all the parts are there, and always have been, but like diamonds on the ground you do not recognise them until you begin to look for them. The Master Jesus didn't leave a Teaching – He just came to show mankind the way and others have written their versions. Maybe it has been necessary for mankind to have something to hold on to and, as I've mentioned before, this is how religion was born, but now there are a few Beings, Muslim, Christian and Jew, who are ready and on their way to identify with an all-purpose philosophy, that acknowledges the Universal power expressed by the soul through the mind to brain consciousness.

As you sit quietly try to establish where this power is in your body. You should begin to have a definite feeling of this and accept where you are on your journey of self-realisation, and build that colour ray that I have already spoken of. Gradually as your true understanding and acceptance of this ray establishes itself, you will begin to feel a slight move onto the next; it all takes time but remember time is man-made, it is non-existent as such in the 4th dimension, so there is no competition or necessity to compete with other Homo sapiens. Unfortunately today, especially in the Western world, this is the order of the day, but remember those that are on the competitive vibration must be left to see the uselessness of it – you are not, or are you? Can you begin to see where all this fits in in the jigsaw of life? How you shed those lower mind ideas? And when you do, you will be a stronger person and perhaps, dare I say, grow up. You can take positive criticism and now, having accepted and reached that certain stage in evolution, see the need of it. But, once more, do not accept negative criticism that is deliberately given to wound you and stop you from moving up that escalator. Once you can truly get on to the Green Ray (Heart) you will be able to let so much go past you as you have accepted an explanation that others, as yet, have not realised.

I'm sure you feel better when you can get some kind of explanation to your questions, whether mental or spiritual, and each of you will, of course, get that revelation in your own way according to the position you have established on the escalator. But as you 'bump' into others you find they too have been searching and find great satisfaction when you come along. Fancy anyone thinking my strange thoughts! How is it they are so similar? Why not? Hopefully you can see why and this enables you to get a greater feeling that it is not your imagination. But what is imagination anyway? Most of your inventors and great writers have used their imagination; some think they have created a great work of art, but as I have mentioned before, many know that the idea has come from some other source. You again will interpret that in your own 'light' of evolution, but it gives you much satisfaction to know that others are thinking likewise.

Chapter 15

LEADING THE WAY HOME

I have taken colour in fair detail as that concerns most of you on the blue/lilac ray; you will then be able to see, hear or know as your Ajna centre lights up. I am very wary of pointing out too much of the spiritual progression of the Being as I fear there will be those who will try to run before they can walk. I again stress all this comes naturally, and when I hear and see Beings being dogmatised into 'Raising your vibration' by means of mantras and various rituals, I shudder for the consequences. The Teachers of the Hierarchy will not abandon you. When they see that light changing and a further development coming forth they will be there – just to pop a word or feeling or thought that you can latch onto to give you a little help to move on up the escalator. The story of the tortoise and the hare comes to mind here – remember which finally got to the winning post.

Now that the 21st century has dawned, much will take place as the planet itself is turning on its axis. Like each one of you, it too has to move on in its contribution to this solar system; and likewise the whole solar system moves on a little further – the Sun takes its children on to touch another tiny piece of the universe, and that touches each planet within its own domain. Naturally you on planet earth will be affected by this through that slightly different vibration. It is all relative.

As the Heart centre (Green/Turquoise ray) gets stronger so does greater desire and understanding. Universal Love will emerge and greater appreciation of the need for a great Teacher to come and round up His children to take them on to the New Age Thinking. There will be upheavals physically, mentally and spiritually – how else can progression take place – towards a greater realisation of the need for the acceptance of the Brotherhood of Man.

May I again point out that these ideas and realisations are for the few, but gradually as the Homo sapiens moves forward, more and more Beings will come into incarnation who are ready and able to take on the teaching of the 4th dimension. The communication of the mind to the brain will be understood and accepted. As man had to battle with the physical in those early years of development so now, having achieved the ability to use the physical in many ways and to a degree understand the how and why of it, the next big understanding has to take place – that of the Mind. How to use it to make the best connection with the brain, to know how to achieve this and so bring the flow of mind power now from the true source in the soul. The few who are touching this realisation of course are finding it very difficult. They are the spearhead of the 21st century spiritual philosophy, but this must surely be the movement forward to bring in the greater love/understanding so necessary for the progression of the planet itself. New Age thinkers and servers are here, and as the planetary vibration increases so more and more souls will be attracted and able to come into incarnation and the world will be able to bring forth the peace and understanding that is necessary for the progression of the countries and planet as a whole.

Think on these ideas, try to realise the pattern that repeats itself through the physical and then the mental; the stronger the thought the stronger the direction from those that have trodden your path and have moved on just a little bit ready to pass on to you their experience and acceptance, as you in turn are passing on your thoughts and experiences to those who are not quite as far up the escalator. Surely there must be a Purpose and a Plan? And once you can see it and hear it, it will give you a reason for the purpose of life itself. Is it necessary, this journey of hardship, frustration and often great unhappiness? These are the parts of the soul that it needs in order to develop its own realisation; special aspects that it can take back 'home' when it leaves this form of experience, the necessary spiritual food to take back to that great pool of wisdom from which it started – perhaps we might call it the Spirit of God/Universe, ever growing and developing as nothing stays the same, nothing stands still. You then can see you are part of creation, maybe only a touch of it but that little bit of your life on this planet, if you have truly understood and accepted the need for this experience, is the reason why you are here in the first place. Just as the caterpillar is necessary to the butterfly, so is the butterfly necessary to the caterpillar – at this moment of time are you a caterpillar or a butterfly? Or maybe at the metamorphosis state?

When you meet people who have found this Jewel in the Lotus, they have a sense of security and purpose – some on the material existence of life, some on the religious and some on the spiritual. You notice their dignity and serenity and wonder perhaps why you are still fighting and arguing within yourself – how you wish you could find what they have found. But if you'd only sit in the silence and try to open your mind, let the soul/spirit come through, feel the air and hear the sound (could be birds twittering), perhaps think of my explanation of the journey to self-realisation, then just for a second you may feel that peace that must come as you journey up the escalator. The mind must be controlled and told to behave and stop flickering about; it only does this because it can't see where it is going – it is like being in a box and bounced about.

More and more of the 4th dimensional philosophy is coming through now. The planet itself is creating the new vibration that certain Beings have the awareness to pick up. A great step forward is actually taking place, but as with all 'new' ideas there is a downside – the idea of the Brotherhood of Man is about to enter the arena and this will cause unacceptance on the part of those who are not ready for it. Those that prefer to keep to the old form of a past regime will have to revise their understanding of life itself. If handled with acceptance and tolerance, civilizations as you know them will bring together the self-realisation that hopefully you yourself have/will experience, and this time the various cultures will help and co-operate with each other instead of destroying that which has been built up through years of trial and error. Humanity will, on the whole, accept that each Being, each country, has its own understanding according to the stage of evolution it has arrived at; some countries have to learn and understand much more, and we come back to that escalator once again. But this time the peoples within those countries will have a greater say, even if fairly illiterate; they will have seen more of the world through the television, and this will make them ask questions and realise that a different life could be theirs if they could agree within themselves. Tribalism and ritual must go and a more responsible direction be taken now they can see how some nations work, how the ordinary citizen has a broader life, so why not them?

All this must be taken slowly in the hands of wise men, as the people in all democracies learn that the individual must be responsible to himself in giving and taking as he goes along, hopefully moving on to the 4th dimension and learning and experiencing Thought Transference. It takes a while for the Being to accept and understand the true Purpose of an incarnation – really it is to enable the soul to 'come into its own'. It is the experience, and hence the wisdom gained by life within a physical body, that is the needed understanding, and indeed the necessity, for evolution; and hence on release from the physical body, return to the essence of life itself with the wisdom that it has gleaned. Here you can see why the Ancient Egyptians put so much ritual into the soul's journey after 'death'; but I am hoping that as you glean a greater understanding of the Purpose of your life, you will see, by learning through meditation to connect with the mind/soul, that this is the way forward – as the dear little bee goes back to the hive laden with honey it has collected from its journey. It is necessary for it to do this or the hive would not exist; will you have some honey to take home do you think?

As the Piscean Age was the age of development of the brain necessary for the physical advancement of the Homo sapiens, so the Aquarian Age will be the acceptance and development of the mind; this will then enable the brain to bring the Being into the truly spiritual understanding that it has come to experience. Just as your planet at the moment is taking a big step forward in its evolution, so of course the new vibration that it will introduce will affect the Beings on the planet. It too has a path of evolution to experience – contributing its 'honey' to the solar system as a whole. Once more, may I say, as you accept your own understanding and 'know yourself', you will see how each, as part of life whether animal, vegetable or mineral, takes its place in the evolution of the whole – a very simple system once you can accept the whole plan. Also, maybe you can see how necessary and important each Being is to the Whole, and how the perfecting of the Homo sapiens is to the planet itself – the one affects the other. Astronomers found this – not just how the planets performed, but why they were necessary in the first place. All is energy, and energy becomes thought, and thought moves into immaculate conception; hence a spark becomes a concrete form being created from whatever essence or energy it derives.

The human being can hold/attract a little more of the energy of the planet than the animal, vegetable or mineral worlds. Hence it is responsible for the energies of those worlds and why mankind is responsible for the protection of those kingdoms. So if the evolutionary mind/force loses its way, and through selfishness and corruption uses that energy in the wrong way, all that it is responsible for will likewise suffer. You talk of the power of thought, so maybe you can see that you are tapping into the energy of the planet, and in doing so transmuting its essence into the necessary idea needed at that moment in time – whether this be material, religious or spiritual.

I will stress once again that I am giving this teaching to the few who have reached the Turquoise Ray and, indeed, have arrived onto the Blue Ray – that of the deliverance of humanity: the power of the word/speech, the focus of the energy delivering the thought through that word to the Beings in the 4th dimension; each Homo sapiens being able to adjust and deliver that thought transference that will be, must be, necessary for the advancement of the planet, plus the understanding of the mind of God. Once you can accept this realisation, then the whole purpose of your life and understanding falls into place.

At this moment in time the planet is in great need of this understanding. It is crying out for the love of Humanity as it now needs the acceptance of its Purpose in the evolution and progression of its place in this Solar System. All the great teachers that have passed your way are still just as in need of you as you are of them. They know the Plan and the Purpose but realise if evolution is to work with love and understanding you are there to help carry it out. Each of you begins to know that you are part of that great army of spiritual warriors; that as the vibration of the planet changes so you too will change; but if that change comes with self-realisation and some acceptance of the necessity to see your part in the scheme of things, then Humanity will be the winner and a great step forward can be predicted.

At this stage of evolution you ask yourself many questions and often there seems to be no answer, but gradually through contemplation, you can acknowledge that scheme of things and a pattern begins to emerge. Rightly you question, and through the small voice that you have begun to hear, you will get some sort of answer. That answer will be what you as a Being have managed to absorb and understand, at the stage of evolution you have achieved in this incarnation – it will be the vital piece of the jigsaw you will take with you on your journey into the new world which you may call 'heaven'. Like this physical world the next is just as concrete and takes shape in a form that may be different from your understanding of life after 'death' but, needless to say, is there all the same.

Many Beings today are asking these more spiritual questions. Their religious teachers are not answering them – some because they cannot, others because they don't consider it's right for them to know. But mankind is now ready to hear and listen to the next stage in this chronicle and some are demanding it. Hence they will abandon religion and search for a more spiritual philosophy – as I have mentioned before this is difficult to find in a material sense, but easier when contemplation moves into spiritual realisation. In a large number of books written there is reference to this which directs those of you who have been asking these questions with your intellect and education. You are ready/able to absorb some of it, and with discussion with those of like-mind begin to move along this new road to the development of a more integrated human being. You need faith and courage in the spiritual world as you have had in the material. It will niggle at you until you start to tackle this new experience, but it will happen. 'God' moves in His way, His wonders to perform, trying so hard to shift the Beings to move on, and in doing so lets them see that this is the way to bring peace on earth, understanding acceptance of each and everyone's discovery of the way, and the truth that passeth all understanding, realising that people are different and yet the same; seeing the other's point of view and knowing why that person sees it in a different light to yourself (the escalator). This surely stops all argument and aggressiveness – perhaps it is what is really meant by 'turning the other cheek'?

At this moment in time, as the planet moves from one Age to another it is always difficult as the vibration changes, and that takes time to realise and accept the understanding of the mind and use it as the spiritual contact with the universal power – not just as an intelligence in its lowest form 'For thine is the Kingdom, the power and the glory'. Think what you are saying in that great mantra, interpret it as you understand it. Once more may I refer to my analogy of the building of your church/mosque/synagogue. You have now taken the scaffolding away. Will that building stand up or will you still have to keep the scaffolding there (religion)? How do you stand in your own understanding? Not what others say or tell you, but you as an integrated human being? Look back on history and you will see that on the whole mankind has not thought for itself; it has followed the line necessary to a degree in the material sense, but now that has been established a way must be found to direct and guide you as a Spiritual Being – not religious. One that has built your house and can live in it, where emotionalism (solar plexus) has been dealt with and the next centre is being used (heart), and hopefully more are moving in to the understanding of Humanity (throat). See the Purpose and gradually you will understand the Plan.

This has been the whole point of writing this booklet as I have heard so many ask the questions 'Where do I go from here?', 'What next?'. Often when they have touched on various books there seems to be a void. I have wanted to close that gap and perhaps draw a more simple picture just to give a hand, so to speak, to help you over this great jump from religion to spirituality. It's different isn't it? But the one must be accepted and respected before the other can ever hope to gain realisation – we must not run before we can walk. All of this philosophy is necessary in the development of the integrated Homo sapiens, one that can take criticism, make mistakes and pick themselves up without the aid of a psychiatrist, knows where to find the spiritual master and hears and feels that direction through the higher self or soul.

In your holy book reference is so often made to 'The Call'. Even in your own life something happens that changes the whole course of the way you think or are going. So much is put down to co-incidence. But is it? Could it be that tiny inner voice, that has at last got strong enough to be heard, however faint, which is giving you that direction so necessary to the development of you as a Being? We are not talking materialism but spirituality – the need to explore this new road of self – realisation. May I emphasise it is the few who are the spearhead of this new adventure (4th dimension), and as they point the way, as always, others will follow. If you read/listen to conversation often it is moving into this way of listening/ speaking. Others hear and that sets them thinking and their minds will be able to help to influence their way of expression; the mind is gradually being heard and each one will appreciate the 'Voice of direction'. This will give place to a further acceptance and realisation of the understanding of 'Mind over matter', and how evolution takes its turn as you progress up the path of self-realisation and, may I say, Mind control.

Once this great leap forward is accepted, just as the Homo sapiens de-veloped from Apeman – because his spine held a different position where it joined the head, he was able to stand up and use his hands which en-abled him to develop so much more quickly and achieve what materially he has through the ages – now the leap forward is Mind acceptance and how it has contact with the greater Universal power that is the energy that truly directs the planet and solar system (other books mention this). Try to see where you fit in and where you have got on the escalator of spiritual development. See that your life has purpose and plan just as that of the planet – you are part of the planet and without you, to a degree, it could not exist. Here we see the teaching of the Brotherhood of Man, the necessity to see the need to work together and put in your little bit of understanding, which ultimately means the love of humanity and the love and acceptance of that Universal power.

The world has taken a great leap forward since the last war. You are, as Homo sapiens, realising that debate and discussion is the ammunition not bombs – albeit I may note it is the spearhead again, but isn't that in itself a great realisation? Spiritual evolution is the key to all of this, and once you can see and accept it perhaps you will begin to understand how it all fits together. It gives you hope as a Being that it is not just haphazard and that there is a definite pattern and direction in all things. You may have to take a few steps back to reinforce your understanding, but ultimately you will make your way back onto the Path and once again move on and along the road that leads you 'home'.

Now you are moving into a new era with new ideas and standards, but with the knowledge you have acquired in this teaching it should help to make you understand yourself and your relationship in this Aquarian Age. One of the difficult things in life is to try and understand evolution, and the need to make certain changes within yourself, country and the planet. Remember you, as 4th dimensional Beings, are at the spearhead; you will receive the necessary information in inspirational form that is required to push evolution that tiny bit forward, so you must be prepared to stand your ground and be ready for the rejection of your ideas. But if you yourself have understood the Plan and the reason for the need to help those that are just beginning to move up the escalator, what a wonderful help you will be to humanity – now you become the teacher so to speak. More and more Beings will be inspirationally led, you have now grasped what that means – feeling and accepting the power through the head centre. This is not imagination, but a contact with a Being that has trodden your path, learned and moved on to the next understanding of the Purpose of existence.

All of mankind has actually been directed by these Beings; when you are ready, as the saying goes, the Buddha appears, your aura lights up and those of us that are responsible for the advancement of Humanity are able to make that connection. Scientists are finding out a great deal about how the planet earth started and through evolution has achieved where you are today – how the movement of the earth has created the continents, how vegetation has developed, and the seasons been created. This is all part of the slow movement of the planet as a whole and is a separate study and one of great interest and necessity. I would dismiss it as 3rd dimensional, using proof of the findings in the light of understanding the earth itself; but what I am trying to put to you in a similar way is how and where are we going through evolution within the Being itself. To a degree the journey is much the same, but on a different level. This time you are not explaining the concrete in the form of rocks and plants, etc. but you your-self, and the instrument is the Mind. The Mind now not in its material sense but in its spiritual aspect – how it influences the brain from the soul. When are you going to be able to accept that? And how do you contact it?

To many this is all irrelevant, but to you more is required – the how, why and where are your pieces of rock, and you are finding it more and more necessary to explore and battle with these questions. At first man has been attacking it through logic and debate, called philosophy, but now you are feeling there is something else. A different dimension in the Mind has opened up another mansion, as I've mentioned before. I choose to call it Spiritual Philosophy, and this will ultimately take you to, dare I say, God itself.